The Touch of a Man's Heart

By

Katrina Avant

The Touch of a Man's Heart
The Touch of a Man's Heart
*

Katrina Avant
Katrinasworks.com

Chapter 1

Paige sat slumped over at her dressing table sobbing intensely. She couldn't sit upright, because the pain was so bad. Through blinding tears, she attempted to raise her head and look at herself in the mirror, only to look away in disgust and shame.

How could he do this? She thought. How could she not have known?

She sat there wondering how she even made it home. She assured the girls she was capable of driving herself home, but she barely remembered getting into her car, let alone driving it. She was grateful that somehow she managed to get home without crashing. At least that's something, she thought through her grief.

"My God, where does this pain come from?" The weight of that pain caused her to double over and collapse to the floor.

Paige lay there in a fetal position, hugging herself, as if this would isolate her from the hurt. This gesture brought no relief, so she attempted to pick herself up from the floor. But because of her emotional state, coupled with her not eating that day, she became light-headed and slumped back to the floor, this time unconscious. The agony of her shredded heart had become too much.

A short time later, Paige sat up with a start. With her head pounding, she tried to remember why she was lying on the floor of her dressing room. When she remembered, the harsh truth came rushing back violently. The force of that memory caused her to draw her knees to her chest, triggering fresh tears to stream down her cheeks. She still couldn't believe how her life had turned inside out without so much as a warning.

"He never said a word, he never said a word," Paige repeated this mantra again and again. She sat there rocking; trying to figure out what happened. Questioning how things could have gone so wrong, so quickly.

Through her pain, Paige knew she couldn't stay on the floor, she had to get up; she had to get herself together. This time, before attempting to rise from her seated position, she took a deep cleansing breath. Wincing, she pulled herself up gradually. Her head pounded with each movement. Closing her eyes she stood and pressed her back against the wall; trying to recover from the awful feeling in her heart as well as her head. Resting there, she let her mind go back to the point of impact. The point where everything in her world all went to hell.

#

Paige greeted her assistant, when she stepped through the door, into the reception area. "Good morning Andee," Paige Bennett was in a great mood that sunny Friday morning when she entered *Beautiful Colors Designs*, a design company she co-owned with her partner Dani Sinclair. Business was good, life was good.

"Good morning Paige," Andee responded.

"Is Dani around?" Paige asked of her business partner.

"She's is out of the office this morning and will return sometime this afternoon," Andee assured her.

Paige loved Andee like a sister. She was the most efficient employee she and her Dani had.

"Ok. Any messages this morning?"

"Yes, just this one from Justin. He called to say that he would have to push lunch back an hour. Some business he needed to attend to this morning will take him a little longer than expected," Andee informed her, handing her the pink slip of paper, containing Justin's message.

"Thanks, Girl."

Paige took the message, and continued into her office, humming softly to herself. She couldn't wait to see Justin. She had missed him over the past few days.

Business had taken him out of town earlier that week. He had called Paige that morning to announce that he was back and needed to see her. She happily agreed to lunch at their favorite spot later that day.

Paige loved Justin Graham. It had taken her years to let her guard down long enough to date, let alone find someone she could love for the rest of her life. Justin was the one man who was able to capture her heart, after spending so many years in solitude recovering from other failed attempts at love. Just the thought of him made her smile as it always did.

"Oh well, enough daydreaming," Paige said aloud. She plopped herself into her chair to get the day started.

The morning ran smoothly while she made calls, returned emails, and reviewed contracts concerning her business. Twenty minutes before Justin was to arrive to take her to lunch, Andee buzzed her.

"Yes, Andee?" Paige answered preoccupied with a clause in a client's contract.

"Umm…" Andee hesitated. She wasn't quite sure what to say. She had practiced a speech in her head, but once Paige answered, she became uncertain as to how to handle the current situation. But knowing she needed to press forward, she continued. "Paige…there is something that you need to see."

"Andee, if it could just wait a few more minutes. I am trying to finish up before Justin gets…"

Andee swept into the room before Paige could finish her sentence.

"Paige this can't wait," She said while offering her the society page of the morning paper. "I am so sorry," Andee added, slowly shaking her head in disbelief.

Dropping the pen she was using and leaning back into her chair, Paige glanced down at the paper but didn't take it from her.

"What could possibly be so important that you felt the need to draw my attention to it now? And the society page at that? You know I don't keep up with the local gossip," She added with a frown.

"Please Paige take a look. You're going to want to see this," Andee pleaded, shaking the folded paper at her.

Sighing, Paige leaned forward to accept the proffered newspaper and read the headline.

"Local Entrepreneur Weds."

From there her eyes scrolled past the bold headline to where they stopped at Justin's face. There it was. A picture of the smiling couple on their wedding day. Paige threw the paper onto her desk as if it had suddenly become a poisonous snake, just as Justin walked into her office.

"Oh my God." She whispered, horrified at what she just saw.

Justin took one look at the discarded article and the horror displayed on Paige's face quickly switched to damage control. "Paige, let me…" He started.

Andee, recognizing it was her queue to leave, quickly retreated from the room closing the door behind her.

Picking up the discarded paper and flinging it in Justin's direction, Paige screamed, "What the hell is this?" She walked around her desk to stand in front of him. This move reduced Justin into silence.

"What is…this Justin?" Page asked again, pointing at the article that now lay on the floor. "Tell me, tell me now!" She demanded.

Sighing, he lowered his body into a nearby chair with his head bowed. He couldn't look at her. "It's true. I got married," he finally answered. Justin raised his head, to say more, however, before he could open his mouth, Paige slapped him hard across the face.

"You bastard! How could you do this to me?!"

"Paige, it's a long story, and if you would just come with me and let me explain...?" Justin pleaded with hope. He knew how absurd he sounded but he needed her to understand why he did it.

In disbelief, Paige placed her face in the palms of her hands, before responding. "I am not going anywhere with you! You used me! Oh God, you used me." She whispered through her fingers. The reality of the moment had her shaking her head slowly from side to side.

"Paige, listen! It wasn't like that. It's not like that!" Justin vacated his seat and tried to assure her by placing his hand on her arm, only to have her snatch it away from him. Just then, Paige's business partner Dani Sinclair entered the room.

"Justin I think you should leave now," Dani sternly suggested to him. Andee met Dani at the main entrance to relay the horror of what was taking place in Paige's office. Absorbing just enough of what Andee was explaining, Dani pushed past her and marched into Paige's office. She would not let her friend endure another moment of this man's betrayal.

"But I need to explain this to her...she needs to understand," Justin pleaded with Dani.

Dani countered through clenched teeth. "Not now Justin, just leave." Dani pointed towards the open door while she defiantly stared him down. She was hoping he would give her a reason to physically tear into him.

Defeated, Justin turned towards the door. Before leaving, he glanced over his shoulder at Paige, who stood in the middle of the office in stunned disbelief.

Before leaving, Justin left Paige with a parting shot, "Babe, sometimes things happen. Things get out of control. If you want an explanation, you know where to find me."

"LEAVE NOW JUSTIN!" Dani shouted in anger, before shoving him through the door and slamming it behind him. She was furious.

Hearing the door close, Paige collapsed to the floor crying hysterically. Dani quickly knelt beside her, pulling Paige into her arms trying desperately to console her.

After making sure Justin left the building, Andee rushed into the room to help comfort her friend.

"Andee, lock the outer office and tell the others that this is their lucky day. They may go home early…and cancel any appointments or meetings that are scheduled." Dani directed.

"Already done. I knew this would be bad," Andee assured her.

Andee had to almost shove her coworkers out the door. They all heard the shouting and wanted to stick around to have more to gossip about. Andee made sure that didn't happen. As soon as the shouting began, she gathered the workers together and directed them to leave; reassuring the protestors that they would receive a full day's pay.

Dani nodded at her from where she sat on the floor holding onto Paige as she cried. Andee sat down on the opposite side of their friend. Gently, she wiped the tears from her face, while whispering words of comfort, even though she knew Paige heard none of them.

Chapter 2

Justin left the building feeling regretful for hurting Paige. He had no intention of bringing such pain into her life. Sighing heavily, he arrived at his car just as his phone rang. Looking at the caller displayed he saw that it was his new bride—Anastasia.

Sighing again, he answered the phone tightly, "Yes?"

"Well, did you tell your little sweetheart the good news?" Anastasia crowed into the phone.

"Yes Anastasia, Paige knows about our marriage," Justin replied indifferently. Closing his eyes and sighing even deeper, he recalled the event that brought him to this upsetting point.

#

Four days previously, Justin left town for what he told Paige was a business trip. But in reality, he had flown back east to get married. In a way, it was a business trip or business merger, depending on how one chose to look at it. This marriage was anything but a loving affair. Anastasia didn't love him and he sure as hell didn't love her, but the arrangement was necessary for them both to get what they wanted.

When Justin got off the private plane at Raleigh-Durham, airport, the farce began. A limo was waiting to whisk him away to the Stanton family compound. The driver greeted him, congratulating him on his upcoming nuptials, as he took Justin's bags and placed them inside the trunk. Justin acknowledged the man with a tight smile, while his stomach did a flip and tied itself into knots.

The ride to the house was nerve-racking, to say the least. The closer he got to his destination, the more apprehensive he became. Was this really what he wanted? He had asked himself this for the hundredth time. Was this worth losing the only woman he ever loved? The struggle with this question was more difficult. He loved Paige, but there were bigger things at stake than his love for her.

This wasn't a real marriage he mused, shaking his head. Maybe he could convince Paige to stay in his life after he explained to her the circumstances of this arrangement. He foolishly tried to console himself with the fact that she loved him, which for him, translated into an uneasy rationalization that she would forgive him. Comforting himself with this new possibility, Justin closed his eyes and settled himself deeper into the car's expensive leather seats.

Arriving at the main house, the driver stopped and opened the door for him. Stepping from the car, Justin noticed the luxury automobiles and limousines parked along the drive leading up to the house and wondered what was going on. Anastasia never mentioned anything about guests.

As he approached the front door, it was suddenly flung open. There stood his soon-to-be wife, Anastasia Stanton, dressed in the latest and most expensive haute couture.

"Darling," She crooned as she wrapped him in her arms and kissed him passionately on the mouth. Justin frowned.

"Smile darling. We don't want the guests to think this isn't a happy union." She whispered through that cunning smile, that he knew all too well.

Anastasia linked arms with Justin and led him further into the huge mansion, where a number of people were enjoying champagne, an array of hors d'oeuvres, and various other lavish dishes. Once the couple stepped across the threshold of the enormous room, the occupants exploded into applause and well wishes for the "happy couple."

Anastasia escorted Justin around the room, introducing the attendees to her soon-to-be husband. Beaming, Justin found himself shmoozing with the crème de la crème of high society. There were governors, senators, and foreign dignitaries among the guests. All were there to wish them well on their happy journey.

I could really get used to this. Justin thought this, while he shook hands with a prince from a foreign country. As he toured the room with his "fiancée" on his arm, Justin soon forgot about his misgivings, and about Paige.

#

Later that night, he answered a knock at his suite's door.

"Well baby, what do you think so far?" Anastasia strolled passed him without waiting for an invitation.

Turning towards her, he closed the door. Justin took note of what she was wearing. Anastasia was clad in scraps of purple lace, paired with six-inch purple stilettos that would have made Victoria blush. He admired the shortest, laciest, piece of lingerie he had ever seen.

"Well, what did you think about the reception tonight?" She asked of him again.

"I must say It was amazing." I hadn't realized how many well-connected people you actually know," Justin replied with eyes that were still admiring her barely-there attire.

Dismissing the comment with a wave of her hand, Anastasia sauntered further into the suite, settling herself on the room's luxurious sofa. Patting the space beside her, indicating he should join her.

"That's only a fraction of the elite that my family and I are acquainted with. As I told you, the business possibilities for you are endless. This merger that we will conduct tomorrow will bring both of us exactly what we want." And what she wanted was him to be her husband in every sense of the word.

Justin walked across the room and joined her. He took note of her carefully made-up face, the coiffured hair, and the soft swell of her swollen breasts, which were hardly concealed in the see-through teddy.

"Tell me. How did you manage to get to my room in that without being seen?" He asked her, indicating her enticing attire.

"Oh, I just left strict instructions for the servants not to enter this wing after they had taken care of you. You and I are the only ones occupying this part of the house I didn't want us to be disturbed." She said this as she gently settled her hand in his lap, massaging his crotch, through his tailored trousers.

"Justin, I know that we didn't arrive at this point in the conventional matter, but you must agree it's very enjoyable. Am I right?" She added with the lift of a perfectly shaped eyebrow, as she felt his penis spring to life in her palm.

"We can at least be good to each other," She whispered close to his ear.

Justin tried not to think about what had brought them together because the mere thought of it brought him back to Paige. He couldn't help but think about Paige, his beautiful Paige. Pushing her out of his mind, he answered her in a passion roughed voice. Anastasia was a beautiful woman. His traitorous body could attest to that as she continued to knead his erection.

"Yes, I must admit it has been enjoyable," He answered her with a breast in his hand.

The pressure and rhythm to which she applied to his rock-hard penis was driving him mad. With one swift move, Justin lifted Anastasia into his arms and hurriedly carried her to the bedroom, to continue their agreed-upon enjoyment.

\#

Standing in the foyer of the Stanton family church, posing for after-wedding photos, Justin observed his new family, the Stantons. There they were Anastasia's parents, aunts and uncles, and a host of cousins and friends. He was trying to control the knot that had formed in his stomach and asked himself again if he had done the right thing. Justin had always been ambitious and saw himself as a millionaire by the age of forty. He just hadn't imagined, that he would accomplish this much sooner and with little effort, by way of his marriage to Anastasia.

All during the ceremony, he kept thinking about Paige and the hurt that this would cause her. He knew he should have told her before he said the "I do's", but he just didn't know how. How could he look the woman, whom he loved and planned to marry, in the eye and explain all of this? Sensing his agitation, Anastasia had squeezed his hand, reminding him of what was a stake. Bringing his mind back to the current task, Justin made it through the ceremony.

"Well son," Mr. Stanton was speaking to him, "Welcome to our family. I know you will make my little girl very happy." He added this last part, shaking Justin's hand a little too firmly to get his point across. A point

Justin read all too well in the older man's eyes. Eyes that said, "If you hurt my daughter, there will be consequences."

"Yes Justin, welcome. You and Anastasia make a beautiful couple." This was from Mrs. Stanton. Beaming like a proud mother, she pulled him into a tight hug; just as tight as her husband's handshake.

"I can't wait for you two to get that family started. I'm overdue for some grandbabies," Mrs. Stanton added.

Justin forced a smile at this. He always thought he would have had a child with Paige. The thought of having a baby with anyone other than her was too much to think about.

"Come along darling, our guests are waiting. Mother, father we will see you at the reception." Anastasia pulled him towards the white stretch limo.

#

The reception was a blur as the expensive champagne flowed. Justin stayed just on the right side of intoxication, so as not to make a fool of himself or to upset his new bride. After arriving at their honeymoon suite, in the most fabulous hotel in the city, he collapsed on the bed exhausted. Exhausted from all the performing that he had executed during that day. Having to pretend to be in love, and to be thrilled to marry the wealthiest young heiress in the state was tiring.

"I know you were thinking about her during the ceremony," Anastasia stated, as she swept in from the dressing room. She had changed out of her wedding gown and stood before him in nothing but her stilettos and grossly expensive wedding rings that she purchased for herself.

Walking over to the bed where he lay, she added, "You know that you are going to have to tell her. You should have told her before today. It may have unburdened you," She continued while climbing onto the bed beside him.

Justin looked up at her, from underneath the arm he had casually thrown over his eyes. "Anastasia, I don't want to discuss Paige with you. She's off limits."

"I'm just stating, that you have to purge her from our lives, if we are to make this marriage work, that's all."

"Look, I will do what I have to do, so don't worry about it. I will take care of it, as soon as I get back into town. This is not something that you do over the phone," Justin told her irritated.

"You know that if circumstances were different, I would have married her and not you," He reminded her.

"But circumstances aren't *different* and you *are* married to me now. So suck it up and let's make the very best of it. And we *can* make the best of it," She cooed, as she straddled him.

"Now down to the business at hand." She continued, kissing him as she unzipped his fly and reached inside.

Grabbing her wrist, Justin sat up. "We have to set some ground rules for this marriage," He informed his new wife.

"Later," She countered, pushing him back onto the bed. "After we consummate our union." With this, she tore his shirt open; popping studs across the room.

#

And now here he was. Standing outside Paige's building, confirming to his new wife that he had just broken the heart of the love of his life. Justin ended the call without saying goodbye.

Chapter 3

"Did you have any idea?" Andee asked Dani later.

They were sitting in the reception area while Paige slept on the sofa in her office. She had cried herself into exhaustion.

Shaking her head, Dani replied. "No, not a clue."

"What kind of low-life bastard does something like that?" Andee asked just as Paige's office door opened.

Both women turned to see her standing in the doorway, with a plastic smile on her face. Even through her pain, she tried to reassure her friends that she was ok.

"Hey, are you alright?" Dani rose from her chair.

"Can we get you anything? Do something for you?" Andee chimed in.

"I'm ok. I just need to go home, take a hot shower, and lie down for a while in my bed."

"I can take you home." Dani offered.

"No, it's ok. I can get home. I just need some time alone. You both understand don't you?"

They went to her then and hugged her. Promising to check in on her later.

#

Shaking herself out of her reverie, Paige pulled herself together and pushed herself from the wall she had leaned against. She padded into her bathroom, opting for a hot scented bath in her sunken tub, instead of a shower. She placed lit candles on every available surface, creating an atmosphere of peace and tranquility. She hoped the warm lighting and aroma therapy improved her mood.

After undressing and donning a robe, Paige padded into the kitchen for a glass of wine. As she walked back into her bedroom, she started past a mirror, only to stop to take a look at herself. She inspected every inch of her caramel-colored body. Turning left, then right. She was five feet eight inches tall, weighing one hundred thirty – five pounds. Paige knew she had a great body for her age of thirty. She worked out at least three times a week and ate healthily.

Slowly bringing her head up to look at her face. Her oval-shaped face was clear and firm. Her hair was professionally cut and styled. She was told by men and women alike, that she was a beautiful woman. She continued to stare at her image, wondering what it was that turned Justin off, to the point that he would marry another woman. Thinking about Justin, brought new tears to her slightly swollen eyes. Not wanting this, she quickly wiped them away and proceeded to the bath.

Hours later Paige lay in her bed wide awake, mentally revisiting the facts that were revealed. She tried to piece things together, to make some sense of what happened and why. Sighing deeply, she turned over onto her side and let her mind go back to the first time that she met Justin.

#

It was two years ago. She and Dani had just opened their firm *Beautiful Colors Designs*, and were looking to put together the right team for the business. Apart from hiring Andee, whom they both knew from childhood, they had no one. Dani had suggested they hire a security firm, to help with the background checks of their potential employees. They agreed on Justin's security company.

"Paige, you have a Mr. Justin Graham here to see you," Andee announced over the intercom.

"Send him in Andee, thanks." Page was sorting through applicants when Justin arrived. She looked up at a tapping on her open door. In strolled Justin Graham and the man was hella fine. Paige instantly took notice and sat up straight in her chair.

He was at least six feet three, solidly and athletically built. His mocha skin, glowing with health, was almost as smooth as the way he entered the room. He was neatly dressed, in an expensive dark blue suit, and crisp white shirt, paired with a red and blue striped silk tie. Justin's features were set apart, by a neatly groomed mustache, and black brows that framed dark intelligent eyes, which sparkled with confidence.

Paige was mesmerized. As Justin moved deeper into the room, she rose slowly from her chair, taking him in all at once.

Hmm, she thought to herself, *nice*. Remembering where she was and why he was there, Paige snapped out of her assessment of him and extended her hand.

"Hello Mr. Graham, I'm Paige Bennett one of the partners of *Beautiful Colors*."

He firmly took her hand in his and shook it. "Good to meet you, Ms. Bennett."

"Please, call me Paige," she suggested.

"I will if you will call me Justin," he countered.

"Ok Justin, please have a seat," she offered.

"So Paige, could you tell me a little about your company and why you need my services?" Justin asked her after he had gotten settled.

"Well Justin, my partner Dani and I are starting our custom-design business, and we need employees. Our business consists of expert custom home and office decor for a well-heeled clientele. We will require people who are trusted and reliable, and that is where you come in. We will need full background checks on everyone hired for the business and insurance purposes."

As Paige talked, Justin made notes on his iPad, which he retrieved from a leather pouch.

"My firm can certainly help you with that," he concluded after she finished explaining her company's needs.

"I also noticed when I walked in, that you do not have a security system. We can handle that for you as well if you would like?"

"I was unaware that you installed systems too," Paige answered surprised.

"Yes, we are a full-service security company," Justin informed with a smile.

"Well, I'm impressed. So it seems we will be doing business together." Paige smiled back.

#

During the weeks that it took to screen for employees and install a security system for *Beautiful*

Colors, Paige saw a lot of Justin. It seemed he was there at every turn, even though he had employees, who were more than capable of handling the job. Whenever he had a moment, he was in Paige's office looking over applications, reviewing the installation progress, or just hanging out. The constant attention he gave Paige was not lost on Dani or Andee, and they often teased her about it. She immediately blew them off, stating that Justin was just being thorough and that he probably gave that type of attention to all of his clientele.

On the last day of *Beautiful Colors'* security installation, Justin breezed into Paige's office.

"Well Paige, the last of the installation is finished, and you have your staff. So I guess my work here is done."

"I must say Justin I am duly impressed," Paige said smiling.

"I'm happy that I didn't have to do all that work. It would have probably taken me months to put a staff together. I am also grateful that you took time out of your busy schedule to oversee the process yourself. It was very reassuring."

"I do aim to please my most favorite client. The pleasure was all mine," he said while bowing slightly. Paige laughed at his antics.

"There is just one more thing that I need to do." Justin suddenly informed her.

"And that is…?" She asked puzzled.

"Will you have dinner with me? I didn't want to complicate things while the work was being done. But now that it's finished, I would very much like to see you outside of business."

Paige smiled. She was hoping to get to know him better on a personal level and not just business. "I would like that very much, Justin."

Justin released a breath that he hadn't realized he was holding until she said yes. "Well in that case Ms. Paige, would you do me the honor of dining with me tonight? I can pick you up around…say seven?"

"Seven would be great."

"I will see you then." Justin winked at her and left her office just as Dani and Andee were entering.

"Well, it took him long enough to ask you out," Dani commented.

"I agree. I thought the man waited for way too long," Andee added laughing.

"I see you two were ear-hustling at the door," Paige smirked at them.

"Oh, don't worry. It was only this one time. We were wondering why he showed up after the contract had been fulfilled, and he had already been paid," Dani shrugged. "Besides, we were dying to know if he would ask you out." They all laughed.

"Seriously Paige, it has been forever since you have been out on a date." Andee pointed out.

"Yeah, so it was about time that you said yes to somebody, and it didn't hurt that somebody is as good-looking as Justin Graham." Dani pointed out.

"He is gorgeous, isn't he?" Paige agreed.

They all laughed again.

"Ok, ladies. Let's get back to work so Paige can finish early and prepare for her date." Andee said. "Come along Dani."

"I am right behind you."

Paige shook her head at her friend. "Now, what should I wear tonight?" She pondered. She leaned back into her chair for some ideas.

#

Paige and Justin had a wonderful dinner at a local restaurant that they both were familiar with. During dinner, they discussed their businesses, friends and family. She learned that Justin was an only child and that his parents were deceased. He had started his security firm three years ago, after leaving a huge conglomerate to strike out on his own. In his employ, were private detectives, security experts, and what he called computer geeks. He stated that when starting the company, he wanted to cover all the bases in security. A sort of one-stop-shop as he put it.

Paige shared her background with him, mentioning how she, Andee, and Dani had met as children with Andee being the younger of the three. They all had grown up together and remained fast friends. So it was natural, that they would all go into business together. She shared that she was the oldest of four children. She being the only girl. She explained that her brothers lived in other states and that their parents were living their retirement in Arizona.

"Ok Paige, I have been dying to ask you. You mentioned earlier at dinner that you were a little rusty at dating. Why is that?" Justin asked while they were sitting in a park, near the restaurant where they had dined.

"Well, my last relationship was less than desirable. It ended badly and left me with a bad taste for dating. So, I decided to take a break and spend some time reflecting on myself, with what I needed and wanted out of life and out of a relationship."

"So how much time did you spend on reflecting?" Justin asked, genuinely interested.

"If you're asking when was the last time I was out on a date or interacted personally with a man, it's been four years."

Justin's eyebrows shot up at that disclosure. "Wow," he responded, surprised. "That's a long time."

"Well, I wanted to be very sure of myself and what I wanted before I ventured down that road again. Justin, I am passed the casual fling stage, so dating just to be dating is not something that I want to do. I very much would like to be in a relationship that eventually leads to marriage. I do enjoy your company, but if this is not something that you want, I will understand. I don't want to waste my time. Do you understand what I mean?"

"I do understand what you're saying and don't worry. We are both on the same page in this book," he assured her with a smile.

#

Paige cried thinking about that particular conversation she had with Justin on their first date. He led her to believe that he wanted everything she wanted. She remembered how she felt that evening, relaxed and self-confident. He made her believe she could have everything that she ever wanted with him. They sat there in the park on that early fall evening enjoying each other's company, laughing and talking. They were so comfortable with each other, that a photographer working the park that night, had mistaken them for husband and wife, offering to photograph them.

She smiled through her tears when she thought about how Justin had wrapped his arms around her and held her close, while the guy snapped their photo. That night in the park, Paige realized she was falling in love with him. She had released all the pent-up fear, caution, and anxiety, that she had embraced in those four years of solitude.

Chapter 4

After a tumultuous night, Paige woke up the next morning to a bright sun shining day. She got out of bed to open the blinds, but her phone rang as she started across the room. Looking at the caller display, she saw that it was Andee. Dropping back down onto the bed, she clicked the answer button.

"Good morning Andee," She answered.

"Hi, Paige. How are you doing?"

"I feel a little better, but I don't think I will ever feel the same again. I feel as though something is broken inside of me, and it can't be fixed," Paige confided with a sigh.

"I know sis, but it will get better, I promise. Have you heard from him?"

"No, he hasn't called."

"He hasn't called?! What do you mean he hasn't called? This man breaks your heart, and he hasn't called to try to explain, not once?"

"No Andee, not even once. I, like you, expected him to call or come by to explain, but I haven't heard from him since he dropped that little bomb on me yesterday. I know said he could explain but I just wasn't in the right frame of mind to listen. I couldn't concentrate on anything but his betrayal."

"Paige I don't get him. How could he be that deceitful and none of us not pick up on it? I mean, my lying bastard radar must be broken because I can usually detect them a mile away. He got by me."

"He deceived all of us, especially me. I should have noticed or felt something since I was the one dating the man."

"Is there something I can do for you?" Andee asked her with concern. She had enough of focusing on Justin. Her friend was hurting and she wanted to help.

Just then Paige's phone peeped, indicating that she had another call. "Look Andee, someone's on the other line. I'm fine but thanks for asking."

"Ok Paige, I will talk to you later, bye." Andee rang off.

Paige clicked over, "Hello?"

"Hey Paige, it's me checking on you to see how you're doing," Dani answered.

"Hey, girl. I'm good...just trying to put the pieces back together. You know?"

"Yeah, I know."

Paige talked to Dani a little while longer, repeating what she told Andee, before clicking off. Getting up from her bed for the second time, she glanced back, only to recall the memory of the first time she and Justin were there.

#

They had gone out to dinner that night and had come back to her home for a nightcap and conversation. However, as soon as they entered the house, Justin pulled her into his arms and kissed her passionately. Paige had moaned with desire and had wrapped her arms around his neck pulling him closer, savoring and enjoying the kiss. He pulled away to look into her eyes, seeing the need for him staring back at him. He lowered his mouth again, kissing her with a need that equally matched that which he saw. She was the one who pulled away next, but only to take his hand and lead him to her bedroom.

"Come with me," she directed, through a passion-filled voice.

She led him down the hallway to her bedroom, to her bed. Justin lifted Paige off her feet molding her into his body, pressing her into the rock-hard display of his wanting. He moaned loudly when he finally placed her on the bed. Paige lay back pulling him on top of her, bringing his mouth back to hers. Justin, without breaking contact with Paige's lips, started to unbutton his shirt. Just as he was about to undo his pants, Paige broke the kiss.

"Justin wait," she said staying his hand. "I'm sorry, but I don't think that I am ready. I know we have been dating a couple of months, but I need to know that I'm not making a mistake, that this is for real."

Justin stood up and took a step back nodding. "It's ok Paige. I do understand, and I want you to be sure when we do this."

Reaching into his pocket, Justin pulled out red foiled squares. "Here, take these. When you're ready, I want you to come to me." He placed two condom packets in her palm and folded her fingers over them.

"When you're ready." He repeated.

Paige smiled and pulled him onto the bed with her again. They lay there talking for the rest of the night, with Justin holding her in his arms until they both fell asleep.

#

"Wow. That was over two years ago," Paige whispered, shaking her head.

After two years, she felt she should have known the man and what he was about. But obviously she had no clue as to whom she was dealing with.

Sighing, she made the bed and decided that she needed to eat something, although she didn't have an appetite. Walking into the bathroom to take a shower, before preparing breakfast, Paige looked into the mirror at her grief-swollen eyes, much more swollen than the day before. She felt abandoned, used, and alone. She was left wondering how she would ever get through this devastating time in her life.

"Something in me did break," she mused, still staring into the mirror. "Something so significant, that it can't be put back together again."

With that thought, she proceeded to the shower stall.

Chapter 5

Sitting at her bistro-styled table, after finishing a small breakfast of scrambled eggs, toast, and orange juice, Paige contemplated on what to do with her day. It was Saturday, so she didn't have to go into the office. Although she knew she should use the time to catch up on some paperwork, she immediately scratched that idea. She didn't feel up to doing any kind of work. Besides, her mind wouldn't allow it.

She was trying hard not to think of Justin, but her mind had other ideas. She thought about his smile, his sexy smile. The way that he threw his head back when he laughed. She thought about how he held her in his arms. The way that he smelled, his touch. Then she thought of the many times, that he said he loved her, loved being with her. Paige remembered how she felt when he loved her slowly and methodically. How he would look into her eyes. At those moments, she just knew when he said he loved her, he meant it. Now she knew it was all lies. Feeling herself about to shed more tears, she got up to do the dishes and to decide on what to do next.

Finishing the breakfast dishes, Paige decided to get out of the house. She felt shopping would do the trick in dispelling her awful mood. She visited several of her favorite stores and bought a few items. She actually began to feel a little better. Shopping was always fun and therapeutic for her. She enjoyed going from store to store, pulling together outfits and finding bargains. She smiled at being free if it was just for one afternoon.

"Paige!"

Paige heard her name and turned to see who was calling her. "Oh no," she groaned. It was Jean, one of the busybodies from her health club. "I don't need this today." This was the last thing she needed this morning of all mornings, to run into this woman.

"Paige, I thought that was you," Jean panted as she raced over to where she was standing.

"Please God don't let her go there." Paige prayed under her breath. If she read the woman correctly, she had heard yesterday's unfortunate news and couldn't wait to rub it in her face.

God must have been busy at that moment because Jean dove directly into her pain.

"Paige hon. I am so, so sorry to hear about your man marrying someone else. I mean…it must have been just devastating for you. I mean...I'm sure it didn't help that his wife is simply gorgeous, or that she's mega-rich," Jean added with a flutter of her pudgy, ring-encrusted hand.

Well, so much for Jean feeling sorry for her, because that smile on her face said otherwise, Paige surmised. What a bitch, she thought assessing the hateful woman.

Jean was five feet three inches tall, about one hundred and fifty pounds with a head full of someone else's hair. She stood there grinning with red painted clown lips, with her body stuffed in clothes that were too small for her. The woman was in denial of her BMI measurements.

Paige knew Jean never liked her, although she often pretended that she did, especially in the beginning. She was always jealous of her and her friends because she felt that the three of them were a little too high-maintenance. Jean thought that every time they were all in the gym together, they intentionally paraded their perfect bodies around mocking everyone meaning her. Paige saw Jean for who she was; a spoiled, rich, and very insecure woman.

"I mean...since you are THE perfect woman for any man." The hateful woman was saying. "I just don't understand it. Oh well, better luck next time," Jean crowed with a smirk indicating her feyned concern.

"Yes, Jean. We all can't be like you with the wonderful husband and the perfect life." Paige threw back. "Oh, that's right, I forgot. Your husband left you last year, didn't he?"

"Oh, Paige," Jean half laughed. "You know Nicolas wasn't worthy of me. Well, gotta go. I have a hair appointment that I simply cannot miss. Goodbye." Jean air kissed in Paige's direction before waving her pudgy little fingers and strolling off to terrorize someone else.

"What a miserable little bitch." Paige grumbled as she watched Jean scurry from the store, taking with her Paige's desire to shop.

Jean snickered as she left Paige standing there hurt and angry. Her work was done, she concluded, as she walked briskly to her hair appointment a few doors down from the clothing store.

Jean never liked Paige or her "perfect" friends. She felt the women always thought they were better than everyone else with their "perfect" bodies, and "perfect" hair. However, in her eyes they were wrong, and she never passed up an opportunity to stick it to them, especially that Miss Prissy Paige.

Arriving at the hair salon, Jean swept passed the frowning receptionist and headed straight for her stylist's chair. Norma rolled her eyes when she spotted Jean barreling her way. Jean was her most difficult customer. Always demanding hairstyles that did nothing but make the mean-spirited woman, with her round body, short legs, and chubby face, appear even more troll-like. If it weren't for her wealth and socialite status, people wouldn't give Alfra-Jean Wilson the time of day.

"Hello, Norma," she greeted, before plopping into Norma's styling chair. "I need you to work your magic on me today," she added while rummaging through her overly expensive handbag for a photo of a hairstyle she wanted Norma to give her.

"So what do you have for me today?" Norma replied with a frown, just knowing that the woman had a photo of some hideous monstrosity buried in her purse. And not to disappoint, Jean pulled out a photo of a hairstyle that made Norma cringe.

"This is the masterpiece that I want you to create today," Jean informed her with a satisfied smile. "I want to look stunning. I'm celebrating."

Norma rolled her eyes. "Celebrating, what are you celebrating?" Norma asked as she draped her with a towel and shampoo cape. Genuinely curious as to what this awful woman could have going on to rejoice over.

"Oh, you didn't hear? Paige Bennett's man married someone else. It's about time that Princess got knocked down a peg or two. She has been floating around this city as if she had it on a string. Well now everyone knows differently." Jean's grinned with pleasure.

Norma's frown deepened, while she escorted her to the shampoo bowl. She never understood why Jean hated Paige so much. Although Norma had never met the woman, from what she could gather from Jean's mockery, all the drama and dislike radiated solely from Jean.

Still savoring the moment of Paige's discomfort, Jean closed her eyes while Norma massaged her scalp, recalling the first time she met Paige Bennett and her friends.

\#

Dressed in a too-tight red leotard with a waist-length lace front wig perched on her head, Jean was doing her usual flirting, with some of the male regulars at her favorite health spa. She flirted with most of the guys there, but James was her target. Although she was married, she didn't mind a little sum thin', sum thin' on the side from time to time, if she could get it. Lord knows her husband had his side dishes and could care less about what she was up to.

She stood next to James with her hands wrapped firmly around one of his biceps, trying to coax him into meeting her for a drink later, when in walked Paige Bennett. James immediately extracted himself from Jean's grip and swaggered over to greet her, as some of the other men in the place had their own reactions.

Paige, dressed in an oversized gray tank top over a white sports bra, black leggings, and cross trainers, seemed to be annoyed with all the attention that she was receiving. She was tall, beautiful, and well-toned. Her hair pulled back into a ponytail, displayed a face that boasted high cheekbones and smooth, clear, radiant sun-kissed skin.

Jean frowned. Instantly disapproving of the newcomer. She knew her type. It was just a ploy that women like her used to get all the men to flock towards them. Well, she would just show her that she couldn't just walk in there and take over.

Jean hustled over to where James had planted himself to introduce himself to the new woman. She planted herself directly between the two and faced Paige.

"Hi there," Jean greeted with a small artificial smile, offering Paige her hand. "I'm Jean. You must be new here?"

"Hello Jean, I'm Paige." She replied taking her hand.

Jean took this as an opportunity to pull Paige from James. Guiding her away from the unwanted audience.

Jean plastered on her sweetest and best smile. "Now that's better. We couldn't talk with those guys gawking at you as if they've never seen a woman before. You're new here, aren't you?" She asked again. Wanted as much information as she could gather from this woman.

"Yes. I've recently moved into the area and needed to find a good place to work out. I hear this one is the best," Paige replied, looking around the room at the various state-of-the-art equipment.

Jean assumed she was looking over the still admiring men, looking at James.

"Well, I guess it is a great place to work out if you are really into that sort of thing," Jean replied. She gave Paige a once-over; frowning at her well-toned body. *Huh, she's here for one thing and one thing only, and that's to prowl around for men.* At this thought Jean's frown deepened.

Paige didn't notice the woman's change of attitude, because at that moment her friends Dani and Andee had arrived, and she had excused herself to join them. She wasn't the only one to join them. As the two women moved farther into the room, reaching their friend, some of the men joined them also. Each was anxious to get to know the three beautiful women.

At that very moment, Jean found hatred in her heart for the women, especially Paige. After Paige arrived that day, James never bothered to give her a second look.

However, that was all in the past now. Jean smiled as she relished the look of hurt on Paige's face.

"Yes indeed," Jean whispered as she enjoyed Norma's soothing shampoo.

Chapter 6

As soon as Paige entered the foyer of her home, her mobile phone rang. "Hello?" She answered.

"Hey girl, where are you?" This was Dani asking.

"Girl I just walked into the house. I was doing a little therapy shopping, and it was working too, that is until I ran into that witch Jean."

"Oh no. I know that couldn't have been pleasant. I'm sure she couldn't wait to rub it in." Dani replied.

"Yes, you know our little Jean." They both laughed.

"But seriously Paige, Andee, and I want to come over and hang out with you tonight. How about it?"

"Sure. I could use the company of my sista girls. Give me a couple of hours."

"Ok, see you in two."

#

"Well, we brought Chinese, Italian, and Thai. Plus your favorite coffee ice cream," Dani announced, holding up the bags she was carrying.

"Oh, oh, and don't forget. We also brought a couple of bottles of wine to top it all off," Andee added displaying her bags.

"Well, I see that you ladies came well prepared. Come on in." Paige gestured, as she moved aside, to allow her two best friends inside. "We can set up everything in the living room."

"Check that. I will just put the ice cream in the freezer," Dani offered; moving towards the kitchen.

"So what did the man have to say for himself?" Andee asked, unpacking the food from shopping bags onto the coffee table.

"He didn't have anything to say, because I haven't heard from him," Paige told her.

Dani came to a dead stop in the kitchen doorway. "What?! Please tell us you're joking."

"Sorry to disappoint you, but I still haven't heard from him. He hasn't placed a call, a text, or an email." Paige shrugged at this bit of news.

"Well damn! Can you believe this shit, Dani? Can you believe this?" Andee huffed.

"Paige, I'm speechless. I mean, I don't know what to say." Dani dropped onto the sofa shaking her head. "I would have thought he would have contacted you by now, with an explanation, as if he could explain something as immense as an entire wedding."

"Well after that revelation, I think we all need a drink. I'll get the glasses," Andee tossed back, as she made her way towards the sideboard to retrieve the wine glasses.

"Here honey, sit down while I fix you a plate," Dani told Paige. "Wow not one word, nothing? The man's behavior is diabolical at this point."

"Here pour her a drink." Andee handed Dani a glass. "What a real bastard," She added, after accepting a glass of wine from Dani.

"I'll drink to that," Paige offered, touching glasses with her friends, before wiping away tears that had suddenly appeared.

Chapter 7

"Come to me when you're ready." Justin was saying.

Paige came awake with a start. She sighed. "It was just a dream,"

Paige had gone directly to bed after Andee and Dani had left. She was mentally exhausted and fell fast asleep. The dream she was having about Justin, felt so real, that she had reached out for him in her sleep.

Paige pushed her hair from her face and leaned over to look at the clock. It was 3:18 am. She sat up and shook her head, wondering when that place inside of her that held all that pain would heal. She could hardly stand it. She lay back down trying to remember the dream in detail, but could only remember bits and pieces of it. Sighing again, she let her mind recall the first time she and Justin made love. He told her to come to him when she was ready, and she had.

#

It was cold and raining that night. Just a few weeks after he had made it clear, that it was her choice, as to when they would make love. She always liked nights like these. They made her feel more alive and more aroused. She had

just gotten out of the shower and was applying her favorite
scented moisturizer to her still-moist body. As she
massaged the cream into her skin, her mind envisioned
Justin's hands performing the task for her. With the rain
tapping against the window, seemingly communicating to
her body, Paige made a decision. This would be the night
she would go to him.

She padded into her bedroom to call him. She
wanted to be assured that he was home and wanted her
company. Justin was overjoyed to hear that she was coming
over. He had expressed that his day had been a long and
difficult one. He needed to see her beautiful, smiling face.

Paige dressed carefully for her first time with him.
She wanted everything to be perfect. She chose the sexiest
red lingerie that she owned. Searching through her closet,
she selected a short, gray sweater dress, that plunged deep
and hugged every curve. After slipping into the dress, she
pulled on a pair of four-inch-heeled, black leather boots.
Next, after fluffing out her curly shoulder-length hair, she
placed large silver hoops in her ears. Deciding that she
needed a little color, she slid a pale pink gloss onto her lips,
all the while checking her appearance in the full-length
mirror. To complete the ensemble, she shrugged on a black
hooded trench coat.

Learning of Justin's problematical day, Paige had suggested a much-needed back rub to soothe his aching spirit. What he did not know, in addition to the massage, was the other treat she had planned for him that night.

Satisfied with her appearance, Paige grabbed her keys and the two condom packets he had given her.

"I'm ready." She nodded at the mirror, before heading out to the garage.

#

Paige rang Justin's doorbell. While she waited for him to answer, she smiled, thinking of the special treat she had in store for him.

"He will be surprised," she whispered knowingly.

Justin greeted her, wearing checkered pajama bottoms and an open bath rope, with heavy wool socks covering his feet.

"Come in baby," he coaxed, opening the door wider so she could enter.

Still smiling, Paige stepped over the threshold, happy to see her man. Justin closed the door, then warmly embraced her. Planting a kiss firmly on her lips, letting her know he was pleased to see her.

"Lady, I am so glad you called. It has been such a long, hellish day and your company is just what I need."

Justin kissed her again, reassuring Paige, that she had made the right choice.

"Well let me see if I can make your night a whole lot better," Paige responded with a wink.

"Just seeing you makes me feel better. Come. Let's sit in front of the fire. Babe, I am in dire need of your magic touch tonight." Taking her hand, he led her into the living room, where he had placed a pallet of multi-colored floor pillows directly in front of the fireplace, along with a large towel and massage oil.

"Would you like some hot cider? I have some warming."

"Mmm…maybe later. Right now, I just want to take care of my man." Paige took off her coat and handed it to Justin.

"Well, don't you look sexy?" Justin grinned, before he left to hang her coat.

When he returned, Paige had sat down in front of the fire. He quickly joined her, removing his robe, so she could soothe his knotted shoulders and neck. He closed his eyes, as her hands spread warm oil across his back and shoulders.

"Mmm…baby that feels good. You do have magic hands," He complimented, enjoying her firm and needed touch.

Paige smiled, as she kneaded his broad shoulders. With each stroke, she loved him with her hands and her heart.

After a few minutes, she asked a dozing Justin, "What if I try a new technique? Maybe it will be a little more therapeutic for you?"

"Anything you do is fine with me." He answered in a contented voice.

Paige leaned into Justin then, to reveal her surprise request into his ear. "Make love to me?" She whispered.

Justin immediately opened his eyes and turned to face her. He saw the desire she had for him, along with the condom packets she held in her open palm. No words were needed. Placing her face in the palms of his hands, he brought her closer to him, to kiss her, to claim her. They both moaned at the contact of their lips. Justin's hands went to her hips, bringing her down with him, on top of him. He kissed her feverishly, barely stopping to breathe. He broke the kiss, only long enough to rid Paige of her dress and boots. With this done, they reached for each other, to build on the fire they had started.

"You are so beautiful," Justin whispered as he took an assessment of her lingerie-clad body. His hands were everywhere at once, freeing her breasts from their restraints and freeing her womanhood from its covering.

With the barriers removed, Justin took each breast in turn, into his mouth. Suckling them to hardened peaks, tasting them, worshiping them. Paige moaned eagerly, when his hand moved farther south, when his fingers delved into what made her glad she was a woman. He inserted two fingers slowly. His fingers moved in a rhythm, that matched what he was doing with his mouth, to her breasts.

"Baby, you are so sexy I can hardly contain myself," he whispered between breasts.

Paige could only respond with moans and shudders. Loving the feel of his fingers and mouth on her skin as they did their work. The more Justin loved her with his mouth and hands, the harder he became. To Paige, it felt as if steel lay between them. Her body began to move on its own, matching the movement of Justin's fingers stroke for stroke. Just when she thought she couldn't handle anymore, he stopped and broke contact only to rid himself of his pajama bottoms and to roll a condom, onto his rock-hard shaft. He covered her with his body, kissing her mouth, her throat, and her breasts, before finally joining his body with hers. With one smooth thrust, he was inside her. Paige let out a cry of pure pleasure.

Justin began to move slowly at first, giving her body time to adjust to him, and him time to adjust to her tightness. "I am so glad that you came to me tonight."

"Oooh…baby you feel so good," he moaned deeply. "I knew that it would be like this," he added as he drew back to plunge deeper.

Paige looked into his eyes as he loved her. Feeling every thrust, as the motion vibrated throughout her body. Justin began to pick up the pace, as the temperature between them climbed. His movements became stronger and faster, as he felt Paige's walls grip him tighter. They moved as one, climbing faster, higher. Paige's head thrashed from side to side, as the pressure built, with her body tightening around him. Sensing that she was near the peak, Justin began thrusting even faster. His body moving, as if it were possessed. They both cried out as they reached the edge and tumbled over.

When it was over, Justin gathered her into his arms and pulled a heavy blanket over them. He kissed her forehead and voiced how much he needed her in his life. With heavy lids, Paige began to drift off to sleep. But not before she heard Justin whisper, "I love you." Smiling, she let sleep take her over.

#

Monday morning came quicker than Paige would have liked. She could have stayed home and worked but felt she had spent enough time secluded behind closed doors. Especially, after spending the weekend reliving the moments, when she and Justin made love.

As she drove to the office, she wondered why Justin never tried to contact her. Why he never tried to explain himself? Even though she dreaded hearing his voice again, she had waited and fully expected, to hear from him at some point, over the weekend. But he never called.

Paige concluded she didn't know the man that she loved. Yes, still loved, despite everything that happened. She just couldn't understand why. Justin stated, that if she wanted answers, she knew where to find him, but it wasn't up to her to right the wrongs. And she wouldn't try.

"It will be a cold day in hell before I contact you again," Paige vowed angrily, as she pulled into her parking space.

Making her way into the building, she greeted Andee as she entered the office. "Hi, Andee. What's going on this morning?"

Looking up from her computer, Andee responded. "Paige, we didn't expect you to come in today. Why don't you take another couple of days off? Go to a spa, pamper yourself; hell take a trip."

"No need," Paige sighed. "I think I would feel much better if I were here working instead of home or anywhere else for that matter."

"Ok girl," Andee replied with a shrug of a shoulder. "I placed your messages on your desk. You can take it easy today. You don't have any meetings or appointments scheduled."

"Thanks. Andee is there a message from…" Paige started. She hated herself for even asking. She promised herself she would put Justin Graham behind her.

"I'm sorry Sis. He hasn't called," Andee answered sadly.

Paige just nodded and forced a smile, before she continued into her office.

Chapter 8

One year later

"Dani, you are a mess with yourself," Paige was saying, laughing at Dani's antics.

"Well, I am just saying. If I have to go on a date with another troll, I will scream." Sitting in Paige's office, Dani was giving her the details of the date she had the night before.

"All the man did was talk about himself all night. Pointing out more than once, how women just loved him. Don't make me gag," she added, rolling her eyes and throwing up her hands.

"He seemed so nice and normal when I met him in the coffee shop last week. I guess I need to just take a break and not date for a while." She had enough of the disappointments of the dating world.

"Well welcome to the club," Paige replied.

"Oh Paige…I'm sorry. I didn't mean to dredge up bad memories."

"Nonsense, I'm fine. It hurts sometimes, but not as much as before. I guess time does heal wounds. Besides, it helped that he never called, that way I didn't have to contend with the lies and manipulations. You know?"

"I just don't get him," Dani said, shaking her head perplexed. "Not one word from him since he breezed into this office and announced that he had married. You would think he would have run you down to explain."

Shrugging, Paige replied, "You would think that would have been number one on his to-do list. But that's just one more piece of that particular puzzle. And I know he's well because busybody Jean makes it a point to keep me up to date on his comings and goings, whenever I see her at the gym."

"Ugh, that woman!" Dani groaned shaking her head again. "Why does she even bother to go to the gym? She has remained the same weight and size since we first met her years ago."

Paige chuckled at that. "You know, I think she only goes to snoop and to cause trouble. Not to mention she's been on the prowl ever since her husband ditched her. I kind of feel sorry for her. As much as she flirts, no one has taken her up on her invites."

"Aside from the men she stalks, I wonder if she harasses anyone else as much as she does us?" Dani asked. She found the woman to be an enigma.

At that moment Andee buzzed in. "Dani you have a call on line two. Mrs. Johnston has some questions about her color scheme…Again."

"Thanks, Andee, I'll take it in my office."

"Are you available for lunch later?" Dani asked Paige.

"Sure, but we both better get to work or there will be no lunch."

"Right." Dani rose from her seat and headed to her office.

Paige settled at her desk, to dig into the pile of paperwork she needed to finish before lunch. She loved her job. Even though she was just as creative as Dani, she preferred to handle the business end of the company, instead of dealing with clients. Dani was much more of a people person than she was. She fed off of the chaos that some of their clients brought to the table. She handled them perfectly, without once losing her cool. A lady to the end, that was their Dani.

Paige often laughed at the thought of having to deal with unruly clients. With her temperament, she would probably sink their business in one fell swoop. She was never that cool under pressure.

After finishing a Zoom conference with one of their suppliers, Paige turned to make notes on some changes, when someone chimed in on Messenger. Assuming that it was Mr. Keyes with another forgotten item change, Paige sighed and turned back to her computer screen.

Thinking she must be working too hard, she closed her eyes and shook her head to clear her mind of what she thought she saw. But when she opened them, it was still there. An instant message from the screen name, JGinc next to a single sentence that asked, "Paige, are you there?"

Just barely above a whisper, she asked, "What the hell could he possibly want?" Paige felt lightheaded. She couldn't believe it. It was Justin.

"Paige," He typed again, "are you there?" The message implied urgency.

Letting her curiosity overrule her head she typed back. "Yes, what do you want? This ought to be good she mumbled." She watched the little dots dance as she waited for an answer.

There was a long pause then, "I want to apologize to you," appeared on the screen.

"Exactly what are you apologizing for?" She typed back quickly.

He typed back, "Honey, for breaking your heart. I am sorry." Before she could reply, he added, "You take care", and signed off.

"What the hell was that?" Paige yelled in frustration. How could he drop in with that cryptic message and then sign off? Paige was furious.

Andee came rushing into her office, at her outburst. She could hear her from her desk.
"Paige, what's wrong?"

"Look at this shit!" Paige spat turning the screen for Andee to see. "What the hell is this?"

As Andee read the messages her eyes widen. "What the hell? What a cowardly goddamn bastard! The nerve of this muth…" Dani's arrival cut off Andee's expletive.

"Hey, hey… I can hear you both from my office. What is going on here? She looked to each woman for the source of their uproar.

"Look at this!" Andee pointed angrily at Paige's monitor.

Dani walked over to Paige's desk and read the messages. "Unbelievable! Is he for real?" Dani asked, rolling her eyes towards the ceiling. "He waits a year, to the date, I might add, to literally pop up out of nowhere?"

"So help me, Paige, you just say the word and I will go over there and personally beat the shit out of him. I mean it Paige, just say the word." Andee was seething with rage as she clenched and unclenched her fists.

Paige took one look at the raging Andee and burst into laughter. Dani seeing the humor in the moment joined her. Andee looked from one friend to the other, then she too broke into uproarious laughter. The three of them had laughed for a full minute before they could bring themselves under control.

"Andee you have always been the ghetto girl out of the three of us," Paige stated, still laughing. "I don't know what I would do without your antics," she added wiping her eyes.

"Yeah well…antics or not, I meant what I said." She huffed, folding her arms. "You just say the word. But seriously, who does he think he is? He has to be a sadistic son of a bitch to pull this kind of crap. Here you are minding your own business and BAM! He pops up on your desktop, after a year of no communication?"

"I agree with Andee. Why now and what is his motivation?" Dani chimed in. "Why those few words and then sign off like that? What was his purpose?"

"Ladies, I wish I knew, I wish I knew." Paige sighed while reclaiming her chair. "If you don't mind Dani, do you think we can take our lunch a little early? I think I need a drink"

"Sure let me grab my purse."

#

"Can I get a margarita on the rocks please?"

Paige stopped a server, who was passing their table. She blew out a sigh, as she tapped on the tabletop.

"Paige, what are you going to do?"

"I don't know Dani. I just don't know. I thought that I was through with that chapter in my life. It's been a year," she said shaking her head. "A whole year to the very day and he just drops in from cyberspace." Paige blew out another frustrated sigh.

"Well, you know for certain he will contact you again," Dani informed her reaching for her water glass. "He was just feeling you out to see how you would respond to him, or if you would respond at all."

Paige looked at her skeptical.

"Hey," Dani added raising a shoulder in a shrug. "I know you may not want to hear this, but why don't you give him a chance and hear him out? This way you get answers and you really can put that idiot behind you. I'm just saying." She shrugged again.

Paige was shaking her head.

"No, listen! You said yourself, that this was a puzzle and you only had pieces. Why not get the entire picture once and for all? Who knows, it may put your mind and heart at ease. You won't know unless you try." Picking up her fork to dig into her lunch, Dani left Paige to her thoughts.

Paige sat in silence; turning over in her mind what Dani had suggested. She wondered if she could be right. Would she finally get the answers that she needed? Or, would it be some sick twisted game that he wanted to play with her? After considering her options, Paige concluded that Dani was right. It was the only way to get the answers she needed. Just as she had made up her mind to hear him out, when he contacted her again, the server delivered her much-needed drink.

After having a satisfying lunch, the friends decided to do some window shopping before returning to the office.

"I know we didn't talk much more about Justin during lunch, but have you decided on what you are going to do?" Dani asked Paige, while she admired a pair of shoes in a department store window.

"Yes. I am going to take your advice, get the answers that I need, and put this thing to rest once and for all. I agree. I do need all the pieces to this annoying puzzle. He owes me at least that much."

"Dani, I loved that man. He was my heart and my hope," Paige added shaking her head.

"You may not believe this right now, but you will find your true heart and hope," Dani assured her. "You are a good person Paige, who deserves the best that love has to offer. Justin just wasn't it. And yes, you will get over him."

Glancing at her watch, Dani noticed that it was getting late. "Oh, we better get back to the office to relieve Andee for lunch."

"Yeah, and knowing her, she's probably camped out at my desk, staring at my computer, just daring Justin to pop in, so she can curse him out with a few threats thrown in."

The friends laughed at this vision of Andee.

#

As suspected, Andee was posted in Paige's office, sitting squarely in front of her monitor. She was eating a sandwich and talking on the phone to her mother, Olivia.

Paige and Dani always know, when Andee is talking to her mother because she gets very animated. Andee and Olivia were two of a kind. Both are involved in some sort of high drama most of the time.

"Ok Mother, I have to get back to work now. Yes, I will tell them hello for you, goodbye." Andee signed off as Dani and Paige entered the office.

"So what did Olivia buy today?" Dani asked.

Olivia and Andee were also notorious shoppers, and whenever either of them scored a particularly good find, they just had to call the other with the news.

"She bought these chocolate suede ankle boots that are to die for, and the best part is, she got them for half off. She would have gotten a pair for me, but as usual, they were out of my size," Andee added disappointed.

"Anything interesting happened while we were out?" Paige asked cautiously.

"If you're asking, if that asshole popped up on your screen again, the answer is no. He must have sensed that I was laying for that ass."

"Girl, go to lunch," Paige laughed. "And take your time. Dani and I can hold down the fort"

"Thanks, Sis. I think I will hit that shoe store to see what treasures my mother missed. See you ladies later." Andee grabbed her purse and headed for the door.

"That girl is nuts," Dani laughed. "I'm going to my office. I have to find those curtains for Mrs. Johnston. See you later"

Paige smiled her response.

Moving to her desk, she wondered about Justin. What did he really want? She replayed the message over in her mind. Why did he wait a year to apologize? And why apologize without giving her an explanation? She agreed with Dani. She felt that he would try to contact her again. She was certain of it. But the question was, when? More importantly, when he did contact her, how was she going to handle the situation?

Paige thought after a year, her heart had let go of Justin. She thought time had put some distance between, what was needed and what was wanted. Needed, was to forget about him, her love for him. But with every day, her heart still loved him, longed for him. What was wanted, was his smiling face before her, telling her that the past events were all some awful nightmare, from which she was finally waking. However, this was not to be. Her heartbreak was no dream. It was very real and very painful.

#

With the workday finally coming to an end, Paige found herself not having accomplished much. Every time her computer chimed, indicating a message, she hoped that it was Justin. She realized that she was anxious to hear from him again. She needed answers, answers only he could give.

Paige settled back into her chair and thought about the article in the society section that started this whole mess. She would never forget the photo of Justin and his new bride. Leaning forward again, she pulled the paper from her desk drawer. Even though it was the catalyst of her heartbreak, she could not bring herself to throw it away.

Rereading the article, it stated the woman Justin had chosen over her, was Anastasia Stanton, a socialite from North Carolina. Mrs. Stanton-Graham, the article boasted, was from old southern money. It informed her that the two met at a business retreat, that her family's company had hosted in Jamaica. She remembered that the paper had also stated, the couple was rumored to be a perfect match by the best of southern society.

Paige recalled that summer when Justin went to Jamaica. He had gone to the retreat to network, in hopes of obtaining a wealthier client base for his company. She remembered taking him to the airport and kissing him good luck with his prospects. She wondered if Justin knew Anastasia Stanton before he went to Jamaica. And if so, had he planned all along to meet her there for a tryst?

Paige looked back at the photo. Anastasia Stanton-Graham was a very beautiful woman. That was one thing nosy Jean had gotten correct. It had been a year since she last held that small scrap of paper, but the feelings of hurt and betrayal were as fresh as if those past events were happening today. Paige stared at Justin's wife, comparing every feature to that of her own. Anastasia was shorter and a little heavier than Paige. Where Page was slim, Anastasia was more curvy. She had long, thick reddish brown hair. Her green eyes sparkled from the color photo in the article. The perfect complement to her light brown skin.

So is that it? Paige mused. Maybe she wasn't curvy enough. Could it be she wasn't light enough, or that she wasn't high society? Maybe it was because she was not wealthy. She gave him the one thing that she had to offer, her love. At the time, she thought it was enough for him. But looking at the situation now, she felt it wasn't. If it had been enough, he would be happily married to her and not Anastasia.

Shoving the piece of paper back into the drawer, Paige locked it and prepared to head home for the day. It had been a trying day. More so, because of Justin's obscure message. She was looking forward to preparing a sumptuous dinner and spending the rest of the evening relaxing with a glass of wine and some soothing jazz. With that settled, she threw her purse over her shoulder and headed home.

Chapter 9

Paige dropped her bag and keys on the entryway table after closing the door. Hanging her coat in the foyer closet, her mouth watered with the anticipation of the dinner she had planned for herself. She liked to cook. The work of slicing, dicing, and preparation of a meal for her, was just as satisfying as eating the finished product. Tonight she had decided on a porterhouse steak, which she marinated the night before. A fresh green salad, grilled asparagus, and cheesy scalloped potatoes, she decided, would accompany the steak. This was one of her favorite meals. Moving towards her bedroom, she stopped to queue some good jazz on her sound system. She then proceeded to her dressing room to disrobe and prepare for a long hot shower.

While showering, Paige began, again to wonder about her body. She let her hands exam every inch, testing for soft spots, that would indicate she needed to spend more time at the health club. Finding none, she was satisfied that her body was not the reason, that Justin chose someone else to marry. She finished her shower and slipped on loungewear, before going into her kitchen to prepare her meal.

With her dinner savored and the dishes done, Paige lounged on her sofa with a glass of red wine listening to music. She felt relaxed for the first time since her cyber encounter with Justin. After a year of picking herself apart, trying to comprehend why things happened the way that they did, she began to accept, that she was not the problem—he was.

Not that they didn't have their issues like any other couple, but when it came to them interacting one-on-one, things were great. She saw Justin as her good friend first. Someone that she could always depend on. They could discuss anything, from world events, to what happened on some silly television show. Paige realized then, that she missed him as her friend more than anything.

She was still reminiscing, when her phone rang. Certain that it was either Dani or Andee, Paige did not bother to check the caller display before she answered.

"Hello?"

"Paige," Justin spoke softly from the phone.

Paige's stomach muscles tightened instantly. He still has that effect on me, she thought, waiting for him to say more.

"Paige." Justin cleared his throat and started again. "I know that I'm the last person that you want to hear from, but I need to talk to you, to explain things. Things are so messed up…I don't know where to begin."

"How about the beginning? That seems like the best place to start. Don't you agree?" Paige countered with a frown.

"Yes, you're right. I would like to talk to you in person. Is it ok if I come by tonight? I owe you so much."

Paige hesitated, not knowing what to say or how to answer. She pondered a few more seconds before she told him he could come over. It was the only way she would finally get the answers she needed.

She hung up, after agreeing to see Justin within the hour. Suddenly she was nervous. What will he say? Will it be enough for her to get past the anguish, that had taken control of her life for the past year? Most importantly, how would she feel when she saw him for the first time since that dreadful day? Even as she asked herself these questions, her body began to betray her. The mere thought of him coming into her home, made her body scream for his touch.

"No!" She sternly told herself. "He's not mine anymore." Then sadly she added, "He was never mine." That thought threw cold water on her body's traitorous actions.

"I'll just keep that thought firmly planted in my mind and that will keep everything in perspective," Paige said, calming herself.

At that moment, her doorbell chimed. With her back straight and head up, Paige vacated her peaceful spot on the couch to answer the door.

There he stood, Justin Graham. The man who single-handedly tried to destroy her. He was dressed in a heavy green cashmere sweater complementing a pair of body-hugging jeans. As always, he looked good.

Paige said nothing, as she sidestepped his attempt to embrace her. She left him standing there in the foyer, as she walked back into the living room. She heard him close her door and followed her into the room. Paige didn't turn around until he was near enough to smell his cologne.

"Have a seat, Justin," she offered, gesturing towards the sofa. She sat in a chair across from him with her feet tucked under her.

"First of all, I want to thank you for seeing me," he began. "I know that you didn't have to agree to see me and that I don't deserve any act of kindness from you," Justin pushed on, hoping to receive some glimmer of warmth from Paige. Seeing none, he sighed and got to the reason he was there.

"I'm sure you're wondering why I asked to see you, so I will just get to the point." He cleared his throat before he continued. "Paige, I don't want you to think that I didn't love you. Although, after all the time that's passed, I'm sure that is exactly what you think. But please believe me I did…I do love you. I never stopped loving you. It's just that the things that have happened, have been so wrong and so unbelievable, even to me."

"How can you sit there and say that you love me when you married someone else, Justin?" Paige asked in disbelief. "And on top of that, I don't hear from you until a full year later. Then you have the nerve to say that the events that happened a year ago are unbelievable to you. How is that possible?" Paige spoke with a deadly calm that even surprised her.

"I know it sounds farfetched, but just let me continue, please."

Paige nodded, indicating that he could proceed.

"Everything started with that damned business retreat in Jamaica," Justin stated, swiping his hand down his face. "That's where I met Anastasia. We, the group that was there for the retreat, were having a great time that week. I had scored some top companies for my business and was feeling on top of the world. That last night before we were to head home, I, and some of my associates, decided to celebrate, so we went to a club that was off from the resort site. We wanted to get a taste of some local flavor. Well, when we got there, Anastasia and some of her friends and business associates were there. I had met her earlier in the week, but we never engaged in a conversation until then. We had a few drinks, danced, and had a good time. She had an early flight out that morning and had indicated that she needed to leave the club. So I offered to see her back to the hotel."

At that point, Justin looked very uncomfortable, which led Paige to believe she knew what was coming next. She braced herself the best she could, hoping that it would not affect her as deeply, because of the time that had passed. At the same time, she knew it wouldn't matter how much time had passed, as long as her heart was engaged in the situation, and it was firmly engaged.

Justin took a deep breath and plowed ahead, dreading what he had to say next.

"When… when we got back to the hotel, I saw her to her suite," he stammered. "I should have left it at that, but she insisted on a last drink before I headed to my room."

All the while he was speaking he held his head down, but when he spoke next, he looked up and directly into Paige's eyes.

"When we entered her suite and I closed the door, she turned to me and kissed me. I don't know if it was the alcohol or the euphoria of the business boosts I had accumulated...I don't know, but I kissed her back."

Justin closed his eyes for a brief moment before he said the very thing that Paige had been dreading hearing, once he started his tale.

"Paige, we wound up in bed. We slept together. All that week I had fended off advances from aggressive women because I knew I had a beautiful loving woman waiting for me at home. But that night before coming back to you, I messed up."

Paige sat there with tears in her eyes, listening to his betrayal. She couldn't understand, how he could have sex so easily with a woman, that he had only supposedly just met. Especially after professing his love for her so many times before. How could he love her and sleep with a stranger? How could he just toss her love for him aside so casually, as if it meant nothing to him?

Paige wiped at her eyes. "Go on, I want to hear it all."

"Paige I'm sorry," he said, leaning over to reach for her. Paige drew away from him. She wouldn't allow him to touch her.

Justin sighed and pressed on. "The moment it was over, I felt terrible. So much so, that I immediately got dressed, apologized to Anastasia, and left. Once I got back to my room, the full weight of what I had done fell on me. I paced and cursed myself the rest of the night. I couldn't believe what I had done. How I had betrayed you, our relationship, and our love for each other. I called you that night, do you remember?"

Paige nodded. "I thought you sounded tired and just assumed that you'd had a long week. I even asked you if everything was ok and you assured me that everything was fine. I even noticed some distance between us for a few days after you got back. You assured me that it was just the new contracts that had you distracted. So yeah, I remember," Paige responded in a sad weary voice.

"Excuse me a minute." Getting up from her chair, Paige walked into the kitchen and poured herself another glass of wine.

"Would you like a glass of wine?" She called from the kitchen.

"Yes please."

She poured him a glass and headed back into the living room with both glasses. Handing him one, she returned to her chair. They both drank from their glasses, not sure what to say. Paige replayed the words of what Justin had just told her over in her mind. She cringed when she came to the part about him kissing HER, him inside HER. Fresh tears threatened to spill from her eyes, but she stopped them in their tracks.

Paige broke the silence. "You said that you had just met her when you were in Jamaica. When did you have contact with her after the Jamaica trip?"

Justin looked up at the ceiling before he spoke as if the answers could be found there.

"You have to understand. When I left Jamaica, I had no intention of ever seeing her again. I threw myself into my work…and into loving you. I did everything I could to make it up to you without actually telling you. When I wasn't working, I was eating, breathing, thinking of you Paige, only you."

"I remember how much attention you gave me." She recalled. "I thought it was just because you loved me and you needed me just as much as I needed you. I felt so special and so loved because you were so loving, so giving. I can't believe all that attention was because you were feeling guilty. I should have known something was wrong, but I trusted you. You never gave me any reason not to."

"Baby listen. I NEVER stopped loving you! It was just a moment of weakness that tore our world apart. A moment that I will regret for the rest of my life."

Ignoring his declaration, Paige asked the question that was at the forefront of this discussion. "So tell me, Justin. Where does the marriage fit into this story?" Paige sensed there was much more to be told.

"After Jamaica, I continued with my life... our life together, until a few weeks later when I learned, what I thought was the end of my indiscretion was not to be so. One day out of the blue, Anastasia called me at my office, saying that she was in town and needed to see me. I told her it wasn't possible and that, what we did in Jamaica was a one-time thing. That it couldn't happen again. Well, that's when she informed me it wasn't as simple as that because she was pregnant."

Justin watched Paige's reaction to this. She looked as if she had just taken a physical blow.

"Oh my God, Justin!" Paige gasped. "You slept with her without using protection?"

"I know... I kick myself daily for my stupidity."

New tears formed in Paige's eyes. This time she let them fall, no longer caring that he saw how much his actions had hurt her. Out of all the things he could have told her, the possibility of a baby never entered her mind.

"Oh my God Justin, a baby? You have a baby with this woman?"

Paige sat there sobbing. She couldn't believe the level of pain that she felt. She thought she had received the total impact of his betrayal a year ago, but after this new confession, she realized that pain had no limits, no boundaries.

Justin sat there watching her in her agony. Knowing that he did this and there wasn't anything that he could say or do to ease her pain. He watched her as she withdrew within herself, crying softly, rocking back and forth. He wanted so much to hold her but knew at that point, she could hardly stand to look at him, let alone let him touch her. He truly loved Paige, and after meeting her, no one could have told him that he would ever be estranged from her. He had no one to blame but himself.

Before he met Paige, admittedly, he had dated many women. He had never found a woman that touched him the way Paige had. He knew when he met her, she was the one. But in the course of dating her, he realized just how special she was. She was the type of woman every sane man spent his life searching for. She was the woman, whom many looked for, but only a few found.

Justin hung his head when he thought of how unworthy he felt at times when he was with Paige. He knew he wanted her, but often wondered if he deserved her. If he was truthful with himself, there was a small seed of doubt deep within him that gave way to the opportunity for his indiscretion. He often wondered if somehow he allowed himself to cheat because of that feeling of unworthiness. He could have just as easily resisted Anastasia, but he willfully chose to sleep with her.

Paige sat there, feeling so hollow inside, asking herself how one indiscretion could cause so much damage. Why did this have to happen? She had waited her entire life to meet someone like Justin. He was her heart, her hope. How could things turn into this awful nightmare?

Gathering all of her thoughts and laying them aside, Paige finally was able to pull herself together enough, to ask him to continue.

Justin explained to her, that because of Anastasia's standing in society, it was not an option for her to become a single mother. He told Paige that he continued to stress his point to Anastasia that it was only a one-time thing. He tried to make her understand, that he was in love with someone else, and that there couldn't be anything other than a child between them. That is if she chose to keep the baby.

"That's when Anastasia informed me, that Stantons did not have abortions and that she was having the baby. She also informed me, that she would not be raising the child alone because Stantons did not do single parenthood under any circumstances." Justin sighed deeply, appearing tired and defeated.

"She threatened to ruin me if I didn't marry her." Justin added, "And she had the power to do it." This last part left Justin numb. The full weight of what he did had come full circle.

Paige studied him. She finally understood. She understood but did not accept his explanation.

"You should have come to me Justin, we could have figured this out together. She had no right to blackmail you into marrying her. But then again, you should not have given her the ammunition to do so," Paige added. She suddenly became very tired, but she knew she had to hear it all, to the very end.

"So you married her and you didn't say one word to me, not until now. So why didn't you contact me before now? Why didn't you come to me before now?" She demanded.

"After I left your office that day, I realized how stupid I was, and that there wasn't anything that I could say that would fix it. Besides, I thought if I just made a clean break and let you think I was a bastard, it would be better."

"But as more time passed, I came to see that you needed the truth and that I was being selfish by not giving you an explanation. Paige, I will say it again. I am sorry. I know that it won't make a difference, but I still love you and I wish it were you I was married to. My marriage is not a happy one Paige. How could it be, when Anastasia and I don't love each other? I am a man living in a hell of my own making."

Paige said nothing. There wasn't anything more for her to say.

"The reason that I waited a year later to try to explain myself…well, it was to give you time to maybe heal. I see now, that it wouldn't have mattered when I talked to you, because hurt is hurt. Time does not make things better when you're in love with someone. I see that now. Please, baby, do not think for one minute that I don't hurt too because I do."

Standing, Justin added, "I've taken up enough of your time, so I will leave. Paige, I will stay out of your life from now on. I want you to be happy. You deserve to be happy. Please don't let my actions discourage you from seeking out the man, that will make that happen."

With this said Justin walked over to Paige and kissed her on her forehead. He looked at her for a few seconds more, before he walked out her door, leaving her to her pain.

Paige couldn't move. Her head was spinning. She was in so much pain and agony that she couldn't begin to sort out her feelings at that moment. She was feeling so much at once. She sat in that spot for what seemed like hours before she got up to lie down in her bed. Once there she let the dam break, crying until she fell asleep.

Chapter 10

The next morning, Paige lay in bed trying to decide whether to go into the office. She didn't want to, but she felt she would only sit around the house feeling sorry for herself if she didn't. She was better than that. The night before had been rough. The worst she had ever experienced. She couldn't believe her life with Justin was over and that there wasn't anything she could do about it. She loved that man with her whole heart. She often fantasized how he would show up one day telling her that it was all a mistake and that he loved her and wanted to marry her. She shook her head at that. Paige knew there could be no more fantasies about Justin of any kind. He was gone for good and she had no choice but to accept it. So with a heavy heart, she got up to prepare for work.

Andee was not at her desk when Paige arrived at the office. She sighed her relief. She wasn't in the mood to talk to anyone at that moment. She just wanted to go into her office and dig into her work, hoping it would take her mind off of her wrecked love life. Sitting at her desk, she sorted through messages Andee left. She saw nothing important until she came to the last one.

"Oh no," She groaned.

Dani had a terrible cold and wouldn't be in the office for a few days. That would not have been so bad if she didn't have to see her clients in her absence.

Mrs. Johnston, their most difficult client, had called twice that morning about a color scheme. Paige was not Dani, who could calmly reassure the clients without problems. She was the one who gladly handled the business end, a balance she was happy with. She just wasn't any good at handling the clients with their issues. But since Dani would be out, that meant she had to wear both hats, until she was able to come back to work. She made a mental note to send her friend a get-well basket later.

"Hey, Paige," Andee greeted, coming into her office. "I can see from that look that you got my message that Dani is out for a couple of days. Sorry, Sis. I know how much you hate dealing with clients, but it couldn't be helped," she added with a shrug.

"Yeah, I know. With these various flu viruses making their rounds, we can't be too careful." Paige sighed.

"When she called in this morning, she sounded terrible. She mentioned she had a sore throat yesterday evening before we left, but she had no idea it was only the beginning of something worse."

"Is Mrs. Johnston the only one that I have to deal with this morning? And what is it with that woman and her colors anyway? Why can't she make up her mind?"

Andee chuckled. "Your guess is as good as mine. Maybe you will have better luck with her than Dani did. And yes that is the only appointment you have this morning but…"

Paige groaned again, laying her head on her desk, waiting for the other shoe to fall.

"…but you have to meet with a new client this afternoon at his office downtown," Andee continued regrettably.

"Oh just shoot me now!" She mumbled. "Do you think we can pour cold meds down Dani's throat and prop her up to do her job?"

They both laughed at that.

"Ok, ok, I'm a big girl. I can handle this," Paige said with fresh confidence. "Who is this new client?"

"His name is Anderson Stone. He is an up-and-coming attorney, who says he is in desperate need of our services," Andee replied.

"Anderson Stone, Anderson Stone." Paige pondered. "Why does that name sound so familiar?"

"It should. He has been in multiple commercials and ads. You know the ones. "Slaying the corporate dragons for the common people," Andee repeated the jargon with pretend seriousness.

"Seriously though, he used to work for a large law firm in Georgia, but he made such a name for himself, that he decided to venture out on his own. And from what I hear, it was the right move to make. The man is phenomenal"

"Well phenomenal or not, I'm still not crazy about meeting clients," Paige replied grimacing.

At that moment, Andee took a good look at Paige for the first time, since coming into her office.

"Paige?"

"Hmm?" She answered while looking at her computer screen.

"You want to talk about it?'

Paige looked up from her screen to look at Andee. "Is it that obvious?"

"Only to me Sis and that's because I know you so well. What happened?'

Paige turned towards her as Andee planted herself on the edge of the desk. Reluctantly, Paige decided to tell her, what had taken place the night before.

"Justin came by last night," She started.

Andee didn't say anything just waited for her to continue.

"He came by to explain to me the reason he married Anastasia Stanton. The short version is, that he slept with her and got her pregnant."

She watched Andee's jaw clench. She could almost see the wheels turning in her head. Paige knew she had to head her off before she went ballistic, so she promised that they would have dinner that evening, and she would tell her the entire tale then. Satisfied with this, Andee left her office, leaving her to prepare for her meeting with Mrs. Johnston.

#

Concluding her meeting with Mrs. Johnston, Paige couldn't believe how well things had gone. She was able to persuade the woman to accept the color schemes Dani had originally chosen for her. Paige had explained to her, that the design was contemporary but classy. Coming from a family with old money, Mrs. Johnston was the poster girl for class. Paige had actually found the woman quite charming, and not the menace Dani and Andee had made her out to be. She left their meeting smiling.

"Now if only my next appointment goes as well," she said to herself, as she hurried to her car to make her meeting with Anderson Stone.

She would meet him at his office to get a feel for the place, take measurements, and get the general layout. Although Paige hated dealing with the clients, she loved this part of the design process. Having a bare canvas to work with, gave her an instant high because the possibilities were endless. She rarely got a chance to become a part of the creating process, but when she did, she jumped in with both feet.

Paige found the address she was looking for and parked her car in the parking complex across the street. As she walked toward her destination, she took notice of the real estate around her. Mr. Stone was in good company with the high-dollar tenants in the area. She was thoroughly impressed.

She rode the elevator up alone, getting off on the fifth floor. She followed the brass wall plaques, that pointed to Mr. Stone's suite of offices. Arriving at her destination, Paige found the outer double doors open and peeked inside. There were several men milling around with boxes and other odds and ends. Paige assumed they were from a moving company because each was dressed in jeans, sweatshirts, and work boots. She knocked on the open door to get the men's attention. They all stopped what they were doing to look at her.

"Excuse me gentlemen for interrupting, but could one of you tell me where I might find Mr. Stone?"

"Who's asking?" One of the men inquired.

"Paige Bennett from *Beautiful Colors Designs*." She answered.

Paige watched the man slowly swagger across the room, while the others continued with their tasks. It took everything inside of Paige not to roll her eyes. She did not come here to be sized up like a piece of meat by the hired help.

"Ok, Paige be nice," She admonished under her breath. This was one of the very reasons she didn't like working in the field—people and their attitudes.

As the man moved closer, she took this time to actually look at him. She found him attractive. He was about her age, around six four, and well built. She assumed his body was built from moving boxes. Her eyes moved from his body to his face, where there was a couple of day's growth of facial hair that framed a strong jawline. His hair was neatly and closely cropped with a slight wave pattern. *He is handsome she conceded.*

Moving even closer, she stared into the most piercing pair of black eyes she had ever seen. She instantly felt a tremor run through her body.

This man could do things to me with just his eyes, she further thought. *Stop it,* she chastised herself. *You're here to see a client not to ogle the help.*

The man stopped short of invading her personal space and reached out his hand. "Hello Ms. Bennett, I'm Anderson Stone."

Although Paige was duly surprised, she didn't show it. She accepted his hand and shook it firmly. Never taking her eyes from his.

"Nice to meet you Mr. Stone, and please call me Paige."

"Paige it is, and I'm Anderson. I was under the impression from your assistant that I would be meeting Ms. Sinclair."

"Dani is my partner. She's a little under the weather, so I'll be handling this job… that is if it's ok with you?" She added hesitantly.

"Sure, that's no problem. I've seen your firm's portfolio and I must say you both do great work. Please join me in my office," he invited, gesturing toward the inner office.

Paige preceded him across the huge outer room and through the doorway of the next. As she walked passed him, Anderson took the time to assess Paige as she assessed him. She was wearing a pair of black dress slacks, paired with a breast-hugging emerald green silk blouse, under a beautifully crocheted short black swing jacket. He admired her figure with the eye of a connoisseur. Anderson's eyes closed briefly as he inhaled a trace of the intoxicating fragrance she wore. Paige, busy looking over the room, had missed his interest in her.

"Do you have any basic ideas for your office, Mr. ...uh I mean Anderson?" Paige asked without turning to face him.

She was in heaven. The things that she could do with this room. She opened a door that hid a fairly large bath that included a walk-in shower. The bathroom was large enough to accommodate most of her rapidly forming ideas. Another door opened into a rather large conference room, pleasing her immensely.

"Not a clue. As you can see, I'm just moving in...", he said, making a sweeping gesture with his hands. "...and this is all the furniture that I have at the moment."

Paige looked to where he pointed and saw a lone chair and card table, which held a laptop computer. *Yes*, she thought nodding slowly, *I will make this place one of my best creations.*

Continuing her assessment of the suite, she made some notes on a pad that she retrieved from her briefcase. She then pulled a tape measure from the case and calculated the length and width of the room. She took several photos and made sketches of the wall of windows that beheld a great view of the river in Anderson's main office.

All the while she worked, Anderson watched her every move. When she bent to inspect the carpet, he closely admired her shapely bottom. When her head was bowed over her pad, he took in the shape of her face and the cut of her hair. This woman fascinated him with the way she moved and the way she looked. She was very professional and very classy. She never batted an eye, when she realized that he wasn't with the moving company. He watched her size him up as he walked towards her. He knew that look, she liked what she saw. He smiled at that. He wondered if she was married. Suddenly realizing that she was speaking to him, he brought his mind back into the room.

"I'm sorry, what were you saying?" He asked Paige.

"I asked, if it were possible for me to see you in your home environment, to get a feel for who you are as a person. I need to do this to build your office around your personality." She repeated.

"Oh. That's not a problem at all. Just tell me when and I will open my home to you," he assured her with a grin.

"Great! Now I just need for you to tell me when you would like for us to start and what the timeline is. Then we can go from there."

Anderson explained to her that, at the time, he was working out of his home office and that he would like to have the office finished in a month if it was possible. His workload was starting to outgrow his home and he needed the space for his assistant to work and for him to meet with clients in a professional setting. His cousin, whom he hired as his personal assistant, was getting tired of working at his dining room table.

Paige assured him that it could be done, provided he gave her full authority to do her job. They made an appointment to meet at his home the following afternoon. Paige would bring the contract, that they had agreed upon then. She scribbled a few more notes, shook his hand, and left.

Anderson sighed as he watched Paige leave his office. The movers had left and he was there alone.

"I guess I need to head home to clean up the place before she gets there tomorrow," He said to the room with a grin.

Chapter 11

"So you mean to tell me that bastard slept with that cow on that Jamaica trip?" Andee was saying after the waiter had placed their food on the table.

Paige met her at their favorite Mexican restaurant after she met with Anderson Stone. She had just finished telling her about Justin's visit from the night before.

"Yep, that's when it all started." Paige nodded her head while taking a healthy sip of her slushie margarita before continuing. "I just don't understand how he could sleep with someone he had just supposedly met."

"The key word is 'supposedly'. I'm not buying it," Andee spoke around a mouthful of salad, punctuating her sentence with the pointing of her fork.

"I mean who does that? I know a lot of men are dogs and all, but that is pretty low even for him."

"Well," Paige was speaking between bites of food, "It doesn't matter now, does it? He's gone, and out of my life forever."

She tilted her head before adding her next thought. "You know…I still love him and it hurts and all, but not as much as before. So I guess I am healing."

"Glad to hear that Sis. But you know what I don't get Paige?" Andee asked, chewing.

"What's that?"

"How did that busybody Jean miss the kid? She couldn't wait to fill you in on everything else that was Justin Graham. How did she miss that? She would have busted a gut to tell you that bit of news."

Sitting back in her chair, Paige answered her. "I thought about that. From what I could gather from the previous information she supplied, she never knew. Anastasia never spent any time in Metro City. She refused to move. Jean said Justin lived here during the week and flew to North Carolina on the weekends because he refused to move his office," Paige shared, shrugging.

"Well, well, well. Something got by nosy-ass Jean. I'm surprised." Andee laughed, giving Paige a high five.

"Ok, enough on those two fools. How did your appointments go today?" Andee was happy to change the subject.

"You know Andee, they both went quite well. I was hyperventilating for nothing. You and Dani made Mrs. Johnston out to be this overbearing monster, but I found the woman quite pleasant. I got her to keep the original color scheme Dani had planned, and she was pleased as punch when I left. The crew will continue work tomorrow and should be finished by the end of next week." Paige took an exaggerated bow at the table, causing both of them to laugh.

"Well, girl you have the magic touch with that one. I've never met the woman, but speaking with her on the phone and hearing Dani's account, I just pictured the Wicked Witch of the West. So hats off to you for getting the job done. Dani will be very pleased." Andee smiled.

"Speaking of Dani, I called her earlier. You were right she sounds awful. I hope she gets better soon."

"Yeah, I hope so too," Andee agreed.

"Now!" Andee continued, rubbing her hands together. "How did your meeting go with Anderson Stone?"

"It was… interesting," was all that Paige could say.

"Interesting? Is that all you have to say, interesting?" Andee asked puzzled.

Before she could reply, the hairs on the back of Paige's neck stood up. She looked at Andee perplexed. Then around the restaurant to see what had gotten her body's attention. Noticing nothing out of the ordinary, she dismissed the feeling and was just about to elaborate on her answer, when she felt heat on her back. She only had to take one look at Andee's face, to know someone was standing behind her. But before she could turn around, she heard his voice.

"Hello Paige, we meet again. Had I known we would end up at the same restaurant, I would have invited you and your friend to dinner." Anderson spoke as he walked into view.

He was doing that a lot today Paige thought, standing near her. "Hello, Anderson. This is my good friend and assistant, Andee Dalton."

Anderson tore his eyes away from Paige to take Andee's hand.

"Ah, I spoke with you on the phone. It's nice to meet the woman behind the voice," Anderson told Andee.

"Good to meet you too, Anderson," Andee replied, then looked at Paige and grinned.

Paige pretended not to notice her and looked up at Anderson. "So I see you like the food here also."

"Yes, it was one of the first places I found after moving here. I must say, the food is quite good. I am always on the lookout for good restaurants. Maybe you can suggest some tomorrow when you visit my home."

"Sure, I can make a list for you." Paige smiled when she answered him.

"Well, it appears my takeout order is ready, so I will let you ladies get back to your meal. Nice meeting you Andee. Paige, I will see you tomorrow afternoon. Good night." With that, Anderson was gone.

Paige took a huge gulp from her drink, all the while aware of Andee's eyes on her. She then picked up her fork and continued to eat her dinner. After a while, Andee did the same. When Paige finally did look up from her plate, Andee was staring at her with a wicked grin.

"Yes Paige, very interesting," Andee commented sarcastically.

"What are you talking about Andee." She asked as if she didn't know.

"Paige, please. The man is a walking billboard for sex and all you had to say was, the meeting was interesting. The images of him in those ads do him no justice. The man is beautiful, if a man can be beautiful, and he likes you."

"How did you get, he likes me out of that brief encounter? You only saw the man for two seconds and you got he likes me out of that?" Paige stated shaking her head.

"Not only did I pick up on that, I also saw that the feeling is mutual." Andee was not about to let her off the hook. She knew attraction when she saw it and Paige and Anderson were beaming with it.

Paige rolled her eyes at that. Although, Andee was right about one thing. She did like him, and more than she should. Could she be right about him being interested in her also? Oh, what was she thinking? She didn't have the desire or the inclination to get involved with him or any other man. Justin made sure of that. Paige was pushing the thought out of her mind when Andee spoke again.

"And what is this about you going to his house tomorrow?" Andee asked with a lifted brow.

"Has it been that long, since I was out in the field, that you have forgotten that I like to see people in their environment when I'm commissioned to do office space?" Paige threw back with a smirk.

"Yeah, I guess it has. I had forgotten about that," Andee answered sheepishly. "Sorry, Sis I was getting ahead of myself. But seriously, don't close the door to the man, just because the last one hurt you. Every man is not like Justin. You deserve to be happy Paige."

Paige only smiled, while she finished her dinner.

Chapter 12

During Paige's drive to Anderson's home, she realized he only lived a couple of miles from her. She couldn't decide if that was a good thing or not. Her night was in turmoil after she and Andee parted ways. She couldn't get Anderson out of her head. Her first encounter with him that day was just what she told Andee— interesting. She could have left it at that if he hadn't drawn that weird reaction out of her at the restaurant. Paige couldn't understand how she felt him in the room, staring at her before she saw him. No one had ever made the hairs on her neck stand out like that.

"What was that?" She whispered.

Granted the man was gorgeous, intelligent, and confident, but she had met men like him before. So what was it about Anderson that made him so different?

#

Meanwhile, Anderson was home pacing, waiting for Paige to arrive.

What was he doing? He asked himself. He had made lunch for the two of them and he didn't know why. He knew the woman was only coming to view his home for ideas for his office, but he couldn't help himself. For the life of him, he couldn't explain why he was so taken with Paige. From the first time he laid eyes on her, he wanted to know her, protect her, and love her. Anderson had been attracted to women before, but never like this. This was different. It was more than just a simple attraction. It was something he couldn't even name. Whatever this unnamed thing was, it had him preparing a meal for a woman, something he had never done before.

The doorbell chimed. Anderson looked around to make sure everything was in its place. He had come home after leaving the restaurant and cleaned the place just for her. Anderson, satisfied with his assessment, hurried to answer the door.

"Hello Paige, won't you come in?"

"Hi Anderson," Paige responded, stepping into his home.

The designer in her took over immediately, as she moved deeper inside the house. When they reached the living room, Anderson helped to remove her coat and left to hang it up. While he was gone, Paige took a more critical evaluation of the room. She saw several things, that in her expert opinion, could be improved upon. But that was not why she was here she chastised herself.

"Paige, I hope you haven't eaten. I've prepared a light lunch for us to enjoy before you get started." Anderson said this with hope in his voice after he returned to the room.

"I…" Before she could finish her sentence, her stomach spoke for her with a rumble. They both laughed. "I guess you have your answer." She followed Anderson into the dining room.

"I thought you said a light lunch?" Paige asked him.

She looked at the table that could have easily been a page out of any home magazine. He had set formal place settings, complete with stemware, silver, tablecloth, and cloth napkins. Lunch consisted of grilled salmon with hollandaise sauce, sautéed spinach, caramelized baby carrots, soft yeast rolls, and iced tea. Just looking at the food, made Paige's stomach sound off again for some attention.

"Here let's get something into your stomach before it starts to rebel," Anderson suggested, moving around her to pull out her chair.

Paige sat down and placed her napkin on her lap. "Everything looks and smells wonderful Anderson. Do you do a lot of cooking?"

Anderson sat down in the chair opposite her before answering her. "Yes. Well, when I have the time. I love to cook. It was one of the things my mom insisted her boys knew how to do. Whereas my brother hated it, I loved it so much, that at one time I considered becoming a chef."

"Good for her! Some parents think cooking isn't an important skill for their sons to learn," Paige replied.

"May I?" He asked, reaching for her hand to offer grace. Paige placed her hand in his, bowing her head, while he said a short thanks for their food.

After the blessing, Anderson sat patiently waiting for Paige's reaction to the meal. He watched while she cut into her salmon and tasted it. He was not disappointed when she closed her eyes and moaned her delight.

"This is so good. You're a good cook Anderson," Paige complimented, before taking another bite of food.

"I'm glad that you approve." Satisfied, he dug into his meal.

During lunch, they discussed their backgrounds. He listened attentively while Paige shared her's with him. He learned about her family, her parents and siblings, and how she and her friends came together to open *Beautiful Colors*. She told him how she rarely worked in the field designing because she felt Dani was more of a people person than she was. Anderson learned when she designed, she preferred not to have to deal with attitudes and indecisiveness, that usually stifled her creativity.

During the conversation, Paige learned that Anderson was the older of two sons, of a single mother, and that he was originally from Arkansas. He told her his mother was a wonderful woman who instilled love, morals, and values into both of her sons. He emphasized that she had been strict, but not overly stern. She made sure, that he and his brother understood the importance of education, reputation, and respect. Anderson explained that they didn't have much growing up, but they had what they needed. Paige concluded as he spoke, that he loved his mother dearly. His eyes sparkled when he spoke of her.

Anderson explained, that his younger brother Jayden, still lived in Arkansas near their mother. Jayden was a firefighter, a job that he loved. Anderson also shared with her, that as a kid, Jayden was rebellious. Always questioning every instruction their mother gave them while growing up. But after witnessing the death of one of his friends, due to gang violence, Jayden finally got the message and turned away from his stubborn behavior. She knew from the expression on his face, that he was proud of his younger brother and that he loved him as much as he loved their mother.

"So what happened to becoming a chef?" Paige asked, between bites of food.

"Well, as I grew up, I became more interested in law, especially corporate law. I was often curious as to how businesses were able to start and grow. What their legal obligations were to their employees, the environment, and vice versa. I kept up with current events a lot. Especially those involving disputes between companies and employees or larger companies and smaller ones. I wanted to learn how the process worked and how I could contribute, and so a litigator was born."

"I am sure that your mother is very proud of you," Paige stated.

"Well let's just say, she talks her friends' ears off about both of her successful sons, as she puts it." Anderson smiled at the thought of his mother. He loved her very much.

Finished with her meal, Paige smiled and stood to start her task. "Anderson the meal was great. I enjoyed every bite. Now it's time for me to get started, if you don't mind?"

"Sure. But before you do, can I interest you in dessert? I made cheesecake," Anderson tempted.

"I'll tell you what. I will have mine to go," Paige answered chuckling.

Agreeing, Anderson began to clear their lunch dishes, while Paige walked through his home making notes and snapping photos using her smartphone. She took note of the dining room first since they had spent most of their time there. Next, she moved back to the living room. She took an evaluation of the room's masculine furniture. Cream-colored leather sofas and chairs, glass and chrome tables, held African statues of tribal warriors and chiefs. She liked this room, but she could see areas where she could add accent pieces with a bit more color and depth.

From there she headed down the hallway to the first bedroom which he had converted into his home office. This room held a large mahogany desk that was intricately carved and stood on claw feet. Paige walked over to the desk touching its surface. The piece was exquisite and looked totally out of place in that room. She pictured it with her mind's eye, in his downtown office, and was pleased by how and where she envisioned it. She could build his entire office around this piece. She made notes as she moved farther down the hallway, only taking a cursory glance into a bathroom and the guest bedrooms. When she came to the master suite, she came to a dead stop just inside the doorway.

The room was masculine but refined. Anderson's bedroom held a king-sized dark iron sleigh bed, covered by an expensive gray, burgundy, and dark blue down comforter. There were multiple accent pillows of darker shades of the comforter's burgundy and blue colors. The walls and carpet were shades of gray, that made the bed stand out like a jewel. The nightstands were of the same iron as the bed but had pecan brown wooden inlays. Along one wall was a highboy of the same wood as the tables. Along another, placed in front of floor-to-ceiling windows, were two overstuffed burgundy chairs, accompanying an exquisite accent table between them. Paige loved this room. She took note of its owner's personal touches, as she moved further inside. The only thing that she could think to improve it, was to add a nice painting above the bed and a couple of shaded lamps.

The bed. Her gaze returned to the bed. Without warning, she saw herself in that bed, lying naked under Anderson, as he moved inside of her. Paige grew warm over that invasive thought. What was she thinking? She was here to do a job. Decidedly, she had spent too much time there. With shame coloring her face, she started backing out of the room. Not thinking about what she was doing, she backed right into the solid wall that was Anderson Stone.

"Oh, I'm sorry. I should have been paying more attention to what I was doing," Paige rapidly explained without fully turning towards him.

Still embarrassed she pretended to be making notes. She couldn't face him at that moment, because she was sure he would be able to read those wayward thoughts on her face.

"No Paige, it was my fault. I should have let you know I was standing in the doorway."

At this revelation, Paige groaned inwardly. How long had he been standing there? Had he seen her reaction to his bed? She hoped not. It was very unprofessional of her, and she needed to get a grip on her reaction to this man. No man had ever had this effect on her, not even Justin. What was he doing to her mind, her body? She needed to get out of there before she made a complete fool of herself. Carefully gathering up her thoughts and placing them firmly behind a locked door in her mind, Paige turned to face Anderson.

"Ok, Anderson. I think that I have gathered enough information to get started on your office. Oh, I want to ask you about the desk in the other room. Do you think that we could use it in your office? And before you answer, come with me." Paige walked back down the hallway to the room that held the desk.

"As you can see, the desk is quite large and overpowers this room. But it would be perfect for your downtown office. I would like to use it as the focal point." Paige stared at Anderson as she waited for his answer.

Smiling he responded. "Well lady, we're on the same page. I was going to ask you if it could be used there. I bought it with my office in mind. I just didn't know if it would fit into your plans or not."

"I see great minds think alike." Paige smiled, pleased that he agreed.

Looking at her watch she added, "Anderson, I need to head to the office and look over my inventory and make some arrangements to get started tomorrow. I'm excited about this project. It isn't often that I get out in the field, as I explained earlier, but when I do, I am at my best."

They walked back to the living room, where Anderson helped her into her coat.

"Here, don't forget your cheesecake," He reminded, handing her a small bag.

Paige grinned accepting the treat. "Not on your life buster. This is one of my favorite desserts. I thoroughly enjoyed lunch, it was a nice surprise. If you hadn't fed me, I don't know when I would have had a chance to eat."

"Now we can't have that can we?" Anderson winked at her, then led her to the front door.

Although she had only been in his home a couple of hours, Anderson instantly felt at a loss as he watched her drive away. Walking back into the house, he thought about the incident in his bedroom, when she backed into him. He knew he should have made his presence known, but he enjoyed watching her unnoticed. Observing her as she made notes, he was very aware of the moment that made her back out of the room.

She was staring at his bed when all of a sudden her body tensed and her breathing became heavier. He watched her fan herself as if she were hot. He knew at once what she was thinking because he was having the same thoughts. They both had envisioned themselves in his bed making love. Just the thought of it suddenly gave Anderson an erection.

Drawing his hand over the top of his head, he walked into his office. He had work to do. He would think about Ms. Paige Bennett later.

Paige continued to chastise herself on the drive back to the office. What was she thinking? The man was a client for heaven's sake. She had no right to be standing in his bedroom, fantasizing about being naked with him in his bed. What was it about Anderson Stone, that made her lose her head? True, the man was drop-dead gorgeous, but she had encountered handsome men before, without going all jelly inside. Justin never made her feel like this. Justin, she hadn't thought about him since meeting Anderson. Even though she had loved Justin, he never made her feel this aware of her body. She never dreamed about him as she had Anderson.

Anticipating her appointment at his home, Paige's mind had taken Anderson to bed with her the night before. She dreamt they were somewhere dancing together, Anderson holding her body firmly against his, as they swayed to the intoxicating music. As he pressed his cheek to hers he spoke softly. His words caressed her ear, making her long for his intimate touch. The dream then shifted and they were in bed with Anderson doubling as her only covering. His body was hard, lean, and rough against her soft, smooth one. In her dream, she had cried out at their joining. Anderson loved her, as if he knew every inch of her body, anticipating her every move. He held her as if his very life depended upon it. The dream was so vivid so real, that Paige experienced an orgasm, that brought her fully awake.

"I have got to stop thinking about that man. He's a client. And even if he wasn't, I am not ready to get involved in any type of relationship with him." Paige was trying to convince herself. The more she tried to put Anderson out of her mind, the deeper he seemed to plant himself. Sighing, Paige pulled into her parking space and got out of the car.

"I'll do this job and get away from him. We don't move in the same circles, so I won't ever see him again." Satisfied with her plan, Paige walked into her building.

Chapter 13

The next morning Paige stopped at the office before she headed to Anderson's office. She found Dani and Andee talking when she walked in. And from the way that they stopped and looked at her, let her know that the conversation was about her.

"Well hello, stranger," Paige said to Dani, going to her to hug her. "It's good to see you back. How are you feeling? I expected you to be out longer."

Dani smiled and hugged Paige. "No need, I'm feeling better. I'm just ready to get back to work. Although from what I hear, you don't need me around here," Dani replied with a raised eyebrow. Andee was just bringing me up to date on the goings-on while I've been out. How in the world did you get Mrs. Johnston to agree to my color scheme when I couldn't?" She asked Paige thoroughly amazed.

"I don't know," Paige shrugged. "She wasn't that difficult to work with. You and Andee made her out to be enormously disagreeable that I planned for a fight. Instead, I found the woman to be quite charming." Paige shrugged again.

"Ok Miss Thing, keep your secrets to yourself." Dani laughed, with Paige and Andee joining in.

"Andee, is there anything important that I need to take care of before I leave?" Paige asked.

"No, you are free and clear today."

"Great! So I guess I will—" Page started.

"Oh no you don't!" Dani interrupted. "You're not going anywhere until you tell me what is going on between you and Anderson Stone."

Paige shot Andee a look that asked, "What tales have you been telling this morning," to which, Andee pretended not to notice. Rolling her eyes at Dani's comment, and Andee's feign of ignorance, Paige considered just what she should tell her friends. To keep them from making a mountain out of a molehill, she decided not to tell them anything.

"There is nothing going on between Anderson and I, despite what Jean number two here, may have you believe," Paige answered, thumbing towards Andee.

"Oh, I am so hurt." Andee laughed at Paige. "How could you compare me to the queen of mean? You know I get my information from the source, my own two eyes and ears."

They all laughed.

"Seriously Dani, there isn't anything going on between Anderson and me. He's just a client like any other. No biggie." Paige added with a shrug.

Dani and Andee looked at each other unconvinced.

Shaking her head, Paige ignored them and proceeded into her office to collect the materials that she needed, before heading over to Anderson's. She felt she couldn't tell them what was going on when she didn't know herself. Last night she had more dreams about him, which was going to make it more difficult to work for him. She was hoping against hope that he wouldn't be there today. After last night's steamy dream rump, she didn't know if she could comfortably look him in the eye, without giving herself away. Every time she thought about him, the thought brought heat to her body. Grabbing what she needed, she walked out into the reception area, to find that Dani had left for her office and Andee was on the phone. Thanking God for small favors, she left the building.

#

When Paige arrived at Anderson's office, her crew was busy with preparations for wall priming and carpet removal. She spoke to her foreman about the plans she had and the timetable for each phase of the project. Assuring her that everything would go as planned, he gave the workers their instructions, leaving Paige alone to work on her laptop. She was just breathing a sigh of relief because Anderson was not in attendance when he stepped through the door. She felt him before she saw him. She was busy entering data when she got butterflies in her stomach. She knew instantly he had arrived.

Paige watched, as he swaggered over to where she was sitting, never taking her eyes off of his. Even though he was smiling, his piercing eyes seemed to say something. What? Paige couldn't quite tell. They seem to be asking a question that only she could answer. Realizing that she was staring, Paige tore her eyes away, afraid that the answer to that question could be found in her own eyes.

"Good morning Paige," Anderson greeted, once he reached her. "I see things are in full swing around here." He continued, giving the workers a casual glance. They were in the inner office where most of the work was being done.

"Hi, Anderson. I didn't think you would be here today. There is not much to see at this phase. We're only at the beginning," Paige assured him with a plastered-on smile.

She tried her best to look normal, and not like the untamed woman that she was in her dreams. However, he was making that very difficult with the way he was dressed. He was wearing a navy blue turtleneck sweater over his broad chest, paired with butt and thigh-hugging Levi's, along with a pair of Timberland boots covering his feet. Her eyes lingered on his jean-covered muscular thighs which happened to be eye level. She had always been a thigh woman. Realizing what she was doing, Paige mentally shook herself, getting her thoughts under control.

"I know. But as I explained yesterday, I am a process man. I like to see how things work, and how they come together. That is if you don't mind?" Anderson asked.

Oh great! Paige thought. *That's all I need, him hovering around. How am I going to get past hi this man, if he's always here?*

To Anderson, she said, "Oh no, I don't mind at all. This way, if you want changes, we can make them immediately, instead of waiting further down the in the process, saving time and your money," Paige added with a chuckle.

"Good. So can you explain what is happening in this phase?"

Paige nodded and turned towards her computer, to pull up her virtual vision for his office. She explained to him what the workmen were doing to prepare the walls and floor for the color and carpet. She went on to explain the other phases and processes, hoping if she did it all at once, he wouldn't bother to show up at every interval. At least, that was what she was hoping.

"So what do you think so far?" Paige asked him.

"Wow, I didn't know that it was that much involved with decorating. I thought you just slapped some paint on a wall, threw some furniture in and it was done. But I see that it is much more complex than that. There was no way I could do this, no way at all." Anderson appeared overwhelmed.

Good, Paige thought. *That ought to do it. Now he will stay away and I can get this done without his presence.* She smiled inwardly at the thought of finishing the job and getting on with her life, without Anderson Stone being a part of it.

The entire time that Paige was explaining the process of creating his office, Anderson was enjoying being near her. Although he was listening to her, he wasn't altogether paying attention. He leaned in closer than he had to, just to feel the essence of her. He took a full inventory of Paige and noted that she was all woman.

In his assessment of her, he noticed that she didn't wear make-up like a lot of women he came in contact with. She didn't need it. He observed that her skin was clear, smooth, and glowing with health. Skin he longed to touch. On her lips, she wore a pale lip gloss that looked natural not applied. Her shoulder-length hair was dark with a hint of red highlights, that perfectly complimented her caramel skin. Anderson inhaled deeply to savor the fragrance she wore.

I could really get into this woman, he decided.

When Paige finished her virtual tour of his finished office, Anderson hated the thought of moving away from her. He wanted to be near her all the time. Not just be near her, but a part of her life. He had spent the night before, wondering what it would be like to be with her, inside her. Would she come apart in his arms as he loved her? Was she a screamer or a silent lover? Anderson longed to discover the answers to those questions.

Although he wanted to get to know Paige in every way, he wasn't sure that was possible. He knew that she was attracted to him, but she seemed to be wearing a stop sign on her chest. She was guarded and at times seemed unsure of herself around him. As if someone had thrown a wrench in the works, which was her life.

He would give her some space for now, but when the job was completed, he would try to get her to open up to him. Anderson wasn't sure he could just let her walk out of his life, without at least trying to know her. And if luck was on his side, claim her as his.

#

The work in Anderson's office went smoothly. Paige was there every day, making sure that nothing would stop or slow down the progress. She wanted to get the job done as soon as possible. Even though she had wanted to do this job without Anderson's presence, she was a little disappointed that she didn't see much of him. After the first day, he only poked his head in a couple of times to check out the progress. After that, he would call her every few days to see how everything was progressing, but that was it.

Paige was doing her final walk-through of Anderson's office when she turned at a knock on the open door. It was Dani. She was disappointed that it wasn't Anderson, but she managed not to show it.

"Hey, girl. I thought I would come by to check out the place," Dani greeted as she came further into the room.

"Wow, Paige. You have outdone yourself. It looks great. I was admiring the outer office, but this is wonderful."

"Thanks, Dani. I was just about to lock up and head home."

"Has Anderson seen the finished product?"

"No, not yet. He's been busy in court all week. He called about an hour ago and said that it would probably be tomorrow morning before he would get here and finish moving his things in. I met his assistant Taylor yesterday and she was very pleased with what she saw. She assured me that her cousin would be too."

"Paige?"

"Hmm?" She replied, enjoying the final view of Metro City's skyline from the wall of windows.

"Are you a little disappointed to be leaving this job?" Dani asked gently.

Perplexed, Paige turned to look at Dani then. "What do you mean? Sure it was fun and I enjoyed it, but I am more than ready to get back behind my desk."

"That's not what I'm asking. I was wondering if you would miss Anderson?" Dani pushed.

"Giving me free rein to do as I pleased, he didn't have to be here hovering for me to do my job. So no Dani, I won't miss Anderson, because I haven't seen him enough to miss him."

"Honey, don't let the past keep you from enjoying the present. If you are attracted to the man, it's ok. You don't have to be afraid," Dani said, trying to reassure her. She wanted her friend to be happy. She deserved to be happy.

"I'm not afraid Dani, just cautious. Given the circumstances, don't you think I have a right to be? I took a chance and look where it's gotten me."

"I know that you were hurt. But Paige, you can't continue to live your life being overly cautious and not taking a chance that you might find real happiness."

Sighing, Paige replied, "I hear you, Dani. Let's just not discuss this now. Why don't you come and see the private bath before we leave."

While the two women were looking over the lavatory, unbeknownst to them, their conversation was overheard. Anderson had gotten out of court earlier than expected and had decided to come to the office after all. He had just stepped into the reception area when he heard his name. Dani had mentioned that Paige had been hurt. So he was right about her being guarded. He wondered by whom and how was she hurt. Somehow, he vowed, he would find out. Turning on his heels, he left before the women realized he was there.

#

The next afternoon Paige was sitting at her desk, when Andee swept in carrying a huge basket filled to the brim with coffees, cookies, and chocolates, among other delectable treats. Paige sat back in her chair as Andee placed the heavy basket on her desk.

"I guess someone was pleased with his office." Andee grinned.

Paige leaned forward to retrieve the card that was attached. Indeed it was from Anderson. Andee stood watching her, curious to know what he had written. Paige took the card from its envelope and silently read it.

"Aren't you going to share?" Andee asked expectedly.

"It's nothing, Andee. It just says that the basket was a thank you for a wonderful job." Paige told her.

Disappointed, Andee grumbled as she left the office. Paige released the breath she was holding and read the card again.

Paige,

I wanted to thank you for the awesome job that you did in creating my office. I greatly appreciate it. On a personal note, I would like to get to know you. Maybe dinner sometime? I hope to see you again soon.

Anderson

Paige considered the last line. Even though she was attracted to him, she couldn't bring herself to be open for more pain. Realistically, she knew all men weren't like Justin, but the hurt cut too deep, to think about letting someone else in. She just couldn't. She would miss Anderson, but she could live without him. Placing the card in the trash can, Paige turned back to her work.

Chapter 14

Paige, Andee, and Dani walked into the ballroom, where the evening's charity event was being held. After their firm, *Beautiful Colors Designs*, Dani and Paige vowed to give back to the community through charitable donations. The charity they chose, was for special needs children, for whom the banquet was being held.

All three ladies looked stunning in their designer gowns. Each dress suited each woman's personality. While Paige and Dani chose understated attire in black, Andee, being the most outgoing of the three, chose show-stopper red. As they made their way through the room, men and women alike, greeted them, admiring their style, elegance, and grace.

After greeting many of the gala's attendants they found their table. The ladies were excited about the upcoming program and the charity's progress over the years. Commenting on those who they saw in attendance, Paige pointed out the mayor and her husband. She also recognized fellow business owners, mingling with doctors, judges, and attorneys. Attorneys— that word made Paige pause, to think about Anderson. She wondered if he was there in attendance.

Paige had mixed feelings about seeing him again. Although it had been a couple of months since she finished his office, she often thought of him, dreamed of him. She had assumed the dreams would have ended, once the job was finished, but they hadn't. If anything they were more vivid and more intense to her disappointment. Paige glanced around the ballroom discreetly, hoping to catch a glimpse of him. Saddened that he wasn't there, she mentally sighed and turned her attention back to her friends.

"Who is that guy standing over there in the east entrance?" Dani was asking.

"I don't know. I've never seen him before, but he looks familiar," Andee answered. "Does he look familiar to you Paige?" She asked.

Paige turned to where her friends were looking and spotted the tall handsome man they were discussing.

He was about six-two, lean, and fit in his well-cut tuxedo. He had a clean-shaven head, and neatly trimmed mustache, that framed sensual lips, that begged to be kissed. He stood in the entrance of the ballroom, as if he had all the time in the world, as if the world waited for his direction.

Yes, there was something familiar about him, but she just couldn't pinpoint it. She was just about to turn toward Andee to answer, when Anderson walked in and stood next to the man, slapping him on the back. Then she knew. He had to be Anderson's brother Jayden. That's why he seemed familiar. At that moment, as if sensing her, Anderson turned and looked directly into Paige's eyes.

Instantly, Paige blocked out everything that was going on around her. She didn't hear Dani and Andee discussing the brothers, nor was she aware of anyone else in the room. Her focus was squarely on Anderson. Their eyes locked and held as the brothers made their way across the room towards their table. Paige hadn't realized how much not seeing Anderson had affected her until he walked into that room. Her heart pounded, as he grew closer, never taking his eyes from hers. His eyes seemed to answer yes to whatever question that hers were asking. She had to tear herself from his gaze, to answer Andee's question.

"Paige, is that Anderson's brother?"

"Good evening ladies," Anderson greeted them before she could answer. "I see we support the same charity." Turning towards his brother, Anderson added, "I would like you ladies to meet my brother Jayden."

Introductions were made all around. And after Paige had given her hello to Jayden, Anderson had her complete attention.

She let her eyes take full inventory of him, from his head down to the black shine on the shoes that he wore. His tuxedo was fitted perfectly to his sculptured frame. His hair and mustache were neatly and freshly trimmed. The man was perfectly groomed and Paige's eyes loved every inch of him.

"Paige," Jayden was saying, "I want to give you your props for my bro's office. I don't know how you did it, but you captured the very character of the man."

"Thank you Jayden, I did my very best," Paige said accepting his compliment.

"I know I have told you before how much I like the office, nevertheless I have to agree with Jayden, it fits me perfectly. You designed it as if you were inside of my head. You have a great talent, Paige." Anderson's compliment was given with an appreciative smile.

Paige could only smile back as she blushed. What was wrong with her? *Get a grip girl,* she chastised herself. She couldn't believe that she was acting like some unseasoned teen. She didn't dare look at Dani and Andee. What must they think of her? Although she need not have worried about Andee, because she was firmly planted in a conversation with Jayden. Dani was another story. She looked at Paige with a knowing smirk, then excused herself to mingle.

Anderson, sitting down in Dani's vacated chair, turned to Paige. "How have you been Paige?" He inquired.

"I've been fine Anderson," she answered.

"I was hoping that I would see you again. Even though our previous encounters were brief, I enjoyed seeing you when I did. I was hoping that we could spend some time together, nothing serious. Maybe we can do dinner or a movie. It's up to you. And before you tell me no, I want you to just think about it a couple of days before you answer. Will you do that for me?"

Paige nodded. "Yes Anderson, I will think about it."

Smiling Anderson rose and motioned to his brother. To Paige, he said, "I would love to dance with you tonight, so please save one for me." Without waiting for an answer, he winked and left to find his table.

At the start of dinner being served, Dani rejoined them. Paige only half noticed, because her mind was four tables over, seated with Anderson. How could she have thought she could put him out of her life so easily? He seemed to creep into her thoughts when she least expected.

She couldn't even sleep without him invading her dreams. She was in trouble and she knew it. The question was, what was she going to do about it?

With dinner finished, and the program ending, the music began. It didn't take long before Jayden made a beeline over to where Andee was sitting. The two sat and chatted as if old friends. Paige could tell that Andee was interested, by the direct attention she gave him. When Andee didn't want to be bothered by a man, she didn't even pretend to listen. Paige smiled at this. Andee played tough on the outside, but she wanted what every woman wanted, a loving relationship.

"So Paige," Dani spoke, grabbing her attention, "Have you given any thought to what you're going to do about your attraction to Anderson?"

Paige took a deep breath and blew it out before answering. At that very moment, she had made up her mind. She would accept his invitation. Besides, it's just dinner.

"I have. He asked me out and I am going to accept."

"Good for you. I am proud of you." Dani was thrilled. "I must admit, I thought you would blow him off and just walk away. Then I saw your face when he walked in, and I knew you couldn't. Please, Paige, don't just accept, give the man a chance," she added while peering over Paige's shoulder.

Paige turned to see Anderson walking towards them. The man doesn't just walk, she thought, he swaggers. Assessing him again from head to toe, she concluded, indeed, that he was all man.

When he reached her, he simply held out his hand and she took it. He led her to the dance floor to join the other couples, who had hit the floor to take advantage of the night's music.

Anderson took Paige into his arms and led her smoothly around the floor. Their bodies fitted together as if by design. She closed her eyes and just floated with him. As they swayed with the tempo, Anderson placed his cheek to the top of her head and hummed along. Paige immediately thought of her dream, in which they were dancing and later ended up in bed. She tried hard to still her heart because it was beating out of control. *Does he feel that?* Before she could look at him, she heard her name.

"Paige? Is that you?" She heard the woman's wretched voice.

Paige stiffened as she silently pleaded, *please not tonight. Dear Lord, not Jean, not tonight.*

Paige looked to her right and there she was, dancing with an elderly gentleman. "Jean," was all that Paige could manage to squeak out.

"Paige, it's so good to see you out and about dear. I was worried about you there for a while. You had stopped attending social functions. I was just saying to my daddy here, that it is good seeing you. I don't think I've seen you out socially since Justin married Anastasia Stanton. I mean, it's just good to see you trying to get on with your life after Justin dumped you and with a new man at that," Jean ended with a nasty smirk.

"Excuse me, Anderson, I'm not feeling well. I think I should leave."

Without waiting for him to answer, Paige rushed off the dance floor towards her table to gather her things. She didn't see the cold hard glare, that Anderson gave Jean before he left to catch up to her.

"Paige wait!" Anderson called as he reached her.

"What's wrong?" Dani asked alarmed, with her gaze swinging from one to the other.

Andee and Jayden had moved their conversation to the outside balcony and were unaware of what was taking place inside.

"I'm not feeling well...could you please take me home?" Paige asked Dani.

"Sure honey, let me just get my—" Dani started.

"I'll take you home Paige," Anderson spoke to Paige, but looked directly at Dani, pleadingly.

"Paige, why don't you go splash some water on your face, then we will get you home," Dani said. She wanted to get to the bottom of what had upset her.

Paige nodded and headed towards the ladies room.

Once Paige was out of earshot, Dani turned to Anderson for an explanation. "What happened?"

"We were dancing, when this Jean person said something to upset her." He too wanted to understand what exactly distressed Paige. He was furious with the woman who caused her so much discomfort.

Dani closed her eyes, sighed, and counted slowly. When she opened them she saw that Anderson was waiting for an explanation.

"The short of it is, Jean hates Paige. Something happened a year ago, that devastated her, and Jean likes to rub her nose in it. Anderson, I can't tell you any more than that. Paige will have to be the one to give you the full story if she chooses to."

Pulling a keyring from his pocket, Anderson detached and handed her one.

"Here. Could you give this to my brother and explain that I needed to take Paige home?"

Dani nodded. "I will make sure he gets home. Just go take care of my girl."

Anderson offered Dani a reassuring nod before leaving to find Paige.

Paige was in the ladies' room staring at her face in the mirror. Why must that woman be so hateful she thought? Paige had never done anything to Jean to warrant this kind of behavior from her. Was the woman mental or was it just plain old jealousy? She knew she shouldn't let Jean get to her like that, but Anderson didn't know anything about her troubles. If she had made that dig, when he wasn't around, she could have taken it with no problem. But with Anderson there, she feared that he could see her shame.

Pulling herself together, Paige walked out of the ladies' room, to find Anderson standing vigil nearby. She was touched by his concern, but a little apprehensive too. What must he be thinking, from the little that he heard? Did he think her incapable of having a man love her, because

Justin married someone else? She tried to read his expression, but no such luck.

Anderson walked over to where she was standing, clasped hands with her, and declared, "I'm taking you home."

He said it with such authority, that he left no room for argument. She could only follow his lead and hope that she wasn't making a mistake.

#

Anderson left her to her thoughts, on the drive to her home. He didn't ask any questions or make any comments on what happened. He wanted her to tell him in her on time. His thoughts brought him back to the moment that vile woman approached Paige, and how defeated she looked at what was said. Anderson didn't ever want to see that look of despair on her face again. He could wring Jean's neck for putting it there.

He could see that the woman was suffering from self-loathing, with her artificial hair and overly made-up face, amongst other things, but she had no right to inflict that kind of pain on anyone, especially Paige. Anderson wanted to be around to protect Paige, from whatever demons that were haunting her. He vowed he would be by her side to do just that if she allowed him to.

When they reached her home, he was sure she would stop him at the door. But to his surprise, she stepped inside and continued into the house, indicating that he should follow. She took her shoes off, as she headed to her bedroom to place her belongings. Anderson stopped in the living room, where he sat on the sofa, and waited.

A few minutes later, Paige reemerged wearing loungewear and slippers.

"Would you like something to drink?" She asked. He declined so she walked over and sat next to him.

"I'm sure you are probably wondering what that was all about with Jean," Paige stated. Even though she didn't want to she looked at him. He had already witnessed her humiliation. There wasn't anything else to hide.

Anderson didn't say a word, he just sat and waited.

Pulling her feet under her, Paige sat facing him. "Up until about a year ago, I thought I was in a great relationship. His name was Justin Graham, and we had been dating for two years. "This was the man I thought I would spend my life with. But I had to find out in the local society pages, that the man I loved, had married someone else. Up until that point, I didn't have a clue what he was up to. He never said anything to me or gave any indication, that there was someone else. Even though Jean was mean and hurtful, she was right. I had stopped going out socially. Mainly, because I didn't feel up to it, but mostly, because I was embarrassed. I felt whenever anyone looked at me, they saw whatever shortcomings that Justin saw in me. Shortcomings that made him get involved with another woman. I mean, there had to be something wrong with me for him to do that, right?"

Paige looked at Anderson half-jokingly for an answer. What she saw was anger.

"Paige, don't you ever think that was your fault! Do you hear me?!" Anderson was livid.
"Just because that jackass couldn't see the jewel he had, doesn't mean there's something wrong with you."

Anderson couldn't believe that some jerk had the nerve to hurt her like that. No wonder she was guarded. She thought Justin's betrayal was her fault when nothing could be farther from the truth.

"That guy, Justin, has to be certifiable. Paige, you are beautiful, inside and out. There is nothing wrong with you. You just need the right man to love you, yes to love you," he repeated and nodded with a small smile, that softened his face.

"There is no way that man could have truly loved you and done what he did to you."

While he was talking, Paige had hung her head, unable to look at him, not knowing what to think.

"Baby look at me," he coaxed, gripping her shoulders. "Do you understand what I am saying?"

Paige looked up at him then, nodding.

He pulled her close and kissed her softly at first. Detecting no resistance he deepened the kiss, searching for her very being with his tongue. Leaning over her, he guided her backward onto the sofa, lowering his body onto hers. That mere contact brought tears to Paige's eyes. He kissed her feverously, passionately. Paige felt as if she were drowning and being saved at the same time. Her body became his the moment he kissed her. She thought she knew what passion was, but realized she had only scratched the surface until that moment.

Anderson couldn't believe the depths of his feelings for her. Kissing her brought joy to his soul. He had known women before, but never like this. She completed him. She made him want things that he never considered before with any other woman. At that place, at that very time, he knew she was the one that he would love forever.

Breaking contact with her mouth, Anderson sat up, pulling her up with him. He looked into her eyes and saw a life of forever there. He would not take her until she saw the same with him. He told her as much before he kissed her again briefly and left before he broke the promise that he had just made to her and himself. He wanted her, but he wanted all of her because for him this was forever.

Chapter 15

Paige awoke to a ringing phone. She groaned as her hand searched for it on her nightstand. Rising slightly to take a peek at the clock, she groaned again at the time. It was 6:20 am on a Sunday morning. Who could be calling her this early?

"Hello?" She answered with a sleep-coated voice.

"Paige, why didn't you let me know that Jean's spiteful ass was harassing you last night?" This was Andee asking. "Dani told me what happened after we dropped Jayden off. I wish you would have told me. I would have let that heffa have what she's been asking for, for a very long time."

Oh no, armed and ready Andee was at it early. Paige groaned once again. "It's ok Andee. Normally she doesn't get to me, but she just caught me off guard is all. Plus, it didn't help that Anderson was there to witness her foolishness."

"That's all the more reason to give her ass a beat down," Andee reiterated.

"Andee…" Paige started her reprimand.

"Ok, ok, I hear you, Paige." Andee laughed. "So, did Anderson ask what the witch was talking about?"

"Well no. He just brought me home and gave me space. He let me know that if I didn't want to talk about it, it was fine with him. He just wanted to be there for me. I hadn't intended to tell him, but after we got back here, my emotional dam broke so I explained to him about Justin."

"How did he take it?"

"It wasn't what I expected. He was angry. Angry that Justin could do such a thing. Then he kissed me." Paige smiled, remembering that kiss.

"Well whoop-dee-doo! The night wasn't a total loss," Andee shouted excitedly. "Wait until I tell Dani this bit of news. So, is that all you did was kiss?" She asked curiously.

"Andee!" Paige reprimanded her.

"Well, I thought I would ask. The man is fine. But seriously though, you should give him a chance, don't shut him out."

"I know, I hear you. I have agreed to see him, so now you and Dani can dial it back a little ok?" Paige laughed. "I do like him and he seems to be into me, so we will just see how it goes."

"Yes!" Andee exclaimed.

Paige talked to Andee a little while longer, discussing Andee's attraction to Anderson's brother

Jayden. Andee confided that she could get into him under the right circumstances. She told Paige that they talked extensively while they were at the banquet and had agreed to meet for brunch later that day. She was very excited about seeing him again, even though she tried to hide it. Paige was glad for her friend. Andee had dated men who just couldn't handle her strong-willed personality. However, something told Paige that Jayden wouldn't have that problem, especially if he was anything like his brother.

Hanging up from talking to Andee, Paige decided to try to go back to sleep, but no such luck. Every time she closed her eyes, she saw Anderson's face. She felt his mouth on hers, his tongue caressing hers. As her mind savored those thoughts, her body joined in with its own memories. She remembered how her body felt with him pressed against her, how it reacted to his touch.

"Oh, why did he stop?" Paige asked the room. She knew why. He wanted all of her, but Paige just wasn't quite sure she could give that.

Sighing, she turned over trying once more to get back to sleep. Closing her eyes she drifted towards her goal, only to have the ringing of the phone bring her back.

"Oh no, who is it this time?" She asked, a little irritated.

Again looking at the phone's display, it was Dani.

"Andee and her big mouth," Paige grumbled, before answering the phone.

"Hi Dani, I see Andee didn't waste any time."

Dani's laughter greeted Paige. "Yes, you know she couldn't hold that if she wanted to. I wanted to call you last night, but I assumed Anderson had everything under control, and from Andee's account I was right."

"Yes, he took good care of me. He didn't push, he just let me explain in my own time."

"Paige he cares for you. I saw that last night, by the way he looked at you and by how he took control of the situation. And...you didn't see the look he gave Jean when you walked off the dance floor. If looks could kill... For once she actually seemed ashamed of herself."

"Wow, I did miss something. Jean has never been ashamed of anything that she has spewed." Paige was surprised.

"Honey, I am just glad you decided to give the man a chance. He may be good for you."

"I agreed to dinner, that's a start. I don't plan to rush into anything. Although, I didn't with Justin either, and look what that got me."

"Paige you have got to forget about Justin and accept that he just wasn't the right man for you. He didn't appreciate what he had, so now it's time for someone who can, to step into your life."

Paige listened to her friend talk and wondered if Anderson could be that someone. She finally admitted to herself that she liked him and wanted to see where things went with him. She would just be more careful than she was with Justin. She would be certain, that he was the one before she gave her heart. Making the wrong choice again would be too devastating and she didn't know if she could survive another hit like the one she took with Justin.

After assuring Dani, that she would give Anderson a chance to prove himself, Paige hung up and decided to get out of bed. She didn't think that she would be able to get back to sleep after all the early morning phone calls. As she walked into her shower, she thought about Anderson, wondering what he was thinking at that moment. Did he mean what he said last night? Only time would tell.

#

Anderson lay in bed thinking about what he was feeling for Paige. He meant what he told her. He would not take her until she gave all of herself to him. Anderson gladly accepted the fact, that he was committed to proving himself to Paige. There was no turning back for him. He just had to convince her of that.

Thinking back on what she told him, he understood her apprehension. What he couldn't understand was, how any man could just walk away from Paige. Justin must be the king of fools, he thought. Not only was she beautiful, but she was also smart, giving, and kind. And from the way that she responded to him the night before, she was also very passionate. Paige was indeed, the type of woman that any true man would want to spend the rest of his life with. Anderson also understood that he would have to take his time with her. That didn't bother him at all. He lived by the code that, anything worth having was worth working for and waiting for. With this decided, he bounded out of bed, a man on a mission.

Chapter 16

Anderson phoned Paige that afternoon to see if she was up for company. Anxious to see him she invited him over.

Anderson arrived bearing a huge picnic basket of wonderful foods. He had prepared a spinach and shrimp quiche paired with a wonderful mixed greens salad drizzled with his special dressing. There were buttery croissants, and a delicious array of cheesecake slices of chocolate, lemon, and cherry for dessert. His beverage of choice for the meal was a bottle of vintage champagne. Paige was in food heaven.

"Wow! When you said you were coming over, I had no idea you would be bringing a small feast." Paige expressed her joy at his wonderful gifts. She set the table while he unpacked the basket.

"I thought you would like to enjoy a good meal along with my company. Am I right?" Anderson asked with a grin.

"Anderson, with the way you cook, without a doubt your meals are always welcomed."

"Am I always welcomed Paige?" Anderson asked, suddenly becoming serious. "Because I plan to be around a lot… that is if you allow me to be. I meant what I said last night. I want all of you, and as far as I am concerned, I am all in."

Paige didn't know how to respond to that, so she thought a minute before she spoke. "Anderson, you know that I am a little hesitant about getting involved and why." Sensing that he was about to interrupt, she held up her hand to stop him.

"Let me finish. I am attracted to you and I want very much for you to be a part of my life." Inhaling deeply she continued. "So, I am going to take a chance and let you in. But…" She held up her hand again, "…but, we will have to take this slow. I can't go through what I did before with Justin. Do you understand?"

Anderson was thrilled. "I do understand and we will go as slow as you need to. I'm just happy you're willing to give us a chance.

He rounded the table to pull her into his arms to let her know just how much he appreciated her decision. Anderson expressed this by kissing her slowly but passionately.

"Now that is settled, let's eat." Anderson grinned at a pleased Paige.

#

After dinner, Paige and Anderson moved to the living room and spent the rest of the evening in each other's arms, talking and getting to know each other. They shared the small things, such as favorite colors, music likes and dislikes, and birthdates. They also delved into important things, past loves, associations, and most importantly expectations for their relationship.

Paige asked Anderson if there were any women in his past that he may have been close enough to marry. She wanted to get a feel for Anderson's character. She already knew he loved and respected his mother, and that went a long way with her. But she needed more details about his life and past relations to understand him.

Anderson admitted there had been a couple of women in his past that he was close to, but the relationships never got marriage close. He shared with her his last relationship, which ended a couple of years ago, with the woman leaving the country to accept a position, for which she had prepared for most of her life. He explained that even though he cared for her, they both knew that a meaningful relationship was not meant to be. Anderson was just as driven in his career as she was in hers. Therefore, neither of them wanted to make any sacrifices to pursue anything further. They parted as friends. The only other woman that he was close to, was a high school sweetheart, whom he thought at one time they would be together forever. But as they matured and became adults, they realized what they had mistaken for love, was in actuality a comfortable infatuation.

"Cassandra is happily married with three kids living in Florida," he informed her of his high school crush. "So as you can see there haven't been any great loves in my life. Don't get me wrong, I have dated over the years and have met quite a few women, but most never moved past dinner or drinks. I have been so focused on launching and growing my career, that I just haven't made time for a relationship until now that is," he added, smiling at Paige.

"Paige listen. By no means am I or have ever been a womanizer," he continued. "This is all due to my mother drilling it in my head that women, real women are to be cherished. As she put it, women are to be treated like fine China, not to be misused and tossed around. She made it clear to Jayden and me, that we were never to do anything to any woman, that we didn't want done to our mother. That stuck with me."

"You've mentioned your mother, what about your father, is he still alive?" She asked, curious about the omission of his father.

Paige watched a dark expression take over Anderson's face when she mentioned his father. Anderson became quiet as he appeared to struggle with this new topic.

Anderson wasn't stalling. He just didn't know how to deal with the subject of his father. Over the years, he, Jayden, and their mother had gotten used to not mentioning him or thinking about him. It was so natural to leave him out of their lives, that when Paige brought him up, he was caught off guard and just didn't know how to proceed. Anderson hadn't thought about Rendell Stone in years. What's more, he was pretty sure the man hadn't thought about them at all.

Rendell Stone walked out of their lives when his mother Adaisha was pregnant with Jayden. He was six when he overheard Rendell tell his mother, that he didn't want to be a husband or father anymore. He claimed that it was too difficult of a task. He expressed to Adaisha, that he thought he could make it work until she became pregnant a second time. Rendell felt another child was just too much of a burden, too much to endure. Anderson remembered thinking about his mother. If she was able to endure the ups and downs, along with the day-to-day tasks of marriage and parenting, why couldn't Rendell?

His father had worked for the railroad making good money. He had purchased the family home in a good neighborhood. His income had allowed Anderson's mother to be a full-time mom and homemaker, completely eliminating the need for her to work. Adaisha loved her son and husband and spent her time making their home warm, comfortable, and loving. The type of home any husband should have been proud to come home to. But Rendell's job took him out of town most days of the week and he seemed to prefer it that way.

Anderson remembered standing just out of sight, listening to his mother's soft cries, while his father packed a large duffle bag with everything that he could fit into it. After Rendell left, Anderson went to his mother and hugged her while she cried. He hated his father for leaving them, for hurting his mother.

After Rendell left, life changed for Anderson and Adaisha. Even though she was five months pregnant, she had to go out and find a job to support them. Rendell had left them with money to get by for a little while, but Adaisha knew it would not last for long.

Adaisha had worked as an administrative assistant before she met and married Rendell, so she was able to find a job rather quickly. They were able to keep the house for a year until they were forced to sell it and move to a much smaller one in a less-than-desirable neighborhood. Anderson did as much as he could to help his mother, especially when his brother Jayden came along. He knew the situation was a strain for her, but she never showed it and they always had what they needed.

For a while, Anderson believed his father would return and make everything alright again, but he never did. Sometimes he would hear his mother cry late at night when she thought he and Jayden were asleep. This made Anderson hate Rendell even more. His mother was a good and loving woman, who didn't deserve what he did to her. This was why he reacted so strongly to Paige's plight with Justin. He just couldn't understand how some men could hurt the ones who loved them the most.

When Anderson had gotten older, he picked up odd jobs around the neighborhood to help out even though his mother didn't want him to. He felt, that since he was the man of the house, he should help. He didn't know until the day he left for college, that Adaisha had saved every penny he had given her over the years and then some. His mother used the money to set up an account in his name, so he could concentrate on his studies and not have to work until after he received his law degree. His mother was the best.

As Jayden grew older, he became curious about their father, and Adaisha told him the truth. She felt if she made up a story and he found out later, he would think less of her for lying. Besides, his mother always told them the truth about everything. She didn't want her boys to grow up thinking the world was a place to be taken for granted. She needed them to understand that sometimes dreams don't come true. Most importantly, she needed them to understand the world could be a treacherous place, no matter how you moved through it.

After Anderson passed the bar and landed his first real job, he decided to try and find his father. He hired a private investigator, who found Rendell living out west with a woman he met on one of his many trips with the railroad. He dug deeper and learned, that not only was he living with this woman, he had married her and had an entirely new family. He and Jayden had a half-sibling.

He was devastated. His so-called father had left their family to start a new one with a much younger woman, while his mother struggled to keep a roof over his and Jayden's heads. He never told his mother what he had learned. He felt Adaisha had been hurt enough by this man.

Anderson stared at Paige and wondered how he could tell this beautiful, good-hearted woman, that he hated his father and that he wished to never speak of him again. He turned this over repeatedly in his mind, not sure if he should tell her anything. He didn't want to keep any secrets from her, but at the same time, he just couldn't bring himself to go over those very painful memories. They were having such a great time together and he didn't want to taint that with a discussion on Rendell.

"Paige, I…I don't know how to discuss this with you right now. I don't want to hold anything back from you, but I just can't talk about this right now," Anderson answered her, clearly distressed.

"Oh Anderson, I'm sorry. I didn't mean to bring up unpleasant memories for you."

Paige realized she had hit a sore spot with him. She had no idea that a simple question about his father would bring him so much pain. She could see it in his eyes that the pain ran deep.

"It's ok. I will tell you about him, but just not now," he reassured her.

He held her, hoping her closeness would banish the emotions and bad memories that had risen inside of him. He hadn't thought of Rendell in years. He assumed he had dealt with the anger he had for his father years ago, but somehow the man still had power over him and Anderson didn't like that, not one bit.

Paige, wanting Anderson to feel at ease again after bringing up his father, excused herself to refresh their wine glasses. While she was gone, Anderson closed his eyes trying not to recall the day Rendell had walked out on them. He had loved his father as much as he did his mother. But after Rendell left, Anderson found it impossible not to think of the man without anger.

When Paige returned with refreshed glasses, Anderson made a silent vow to make sure that Rendell Stone would not ruin the rest of their evening. He returned the conversation to them as a couple. He was determined to make Paige understand he was not like Justin or his father for that mattered.

Anderson attempted to make it clear to her, that she was the only woman for him and that she didn't have to worry about any other woman invading her territory. He knew it would be difficult for her to accept things with him at face value, but he was prepared to back up every word with his actions.

Undeniably, Paige listened to every word Anderson spoke, trying to gauge his sincerity. She hoped with all her heart, that he was being truthful with her because she knew she could easily find herself falling for him.

Chapter 17

On Monday, Paige strolled into her office feeling better than she had in a long time. Although the weekend had started badly, it had ended with her happy, all due to Anderson. Saturday, after the incident with Jean, Anderson had left her that night feeling like a woman desired. He made it clear, that all she needed was the right man to love her. Then yesterday he made it abundantly clear that he meant that man to be him. Part of her wanted that very much, but the other part of her was terrified.

"Well, good morning Miss. I can see from that smile on your face, that somebody had a good weekend. You are downright glowing." Andee greeted Paige with a knowing smile of her own.

"I can see from that grin or yours, that you enjoyed yourself with Jayden," Paige responded with a raised eyebrow.

"Yes. He took me out to brunch and then we spent the rest of the day at my place getting more acquainted with each other. Not only is the man handsome, he is smart and funny. He kept me laughing. I enjoyed spending time with him," Andee told her, bubbling over with excitement.

"I'm happy for you Andee. You deserve to be happy with someone special in your life. Now that we have two down, we have to get Dani hooked up."

"Hold up and back up! Does that mean you and Anderson are an item?"

Paige nodded grinning.

"Paige I am so happy for you. Dani and I were holding our breath concerning you two. We hoped you wouldn't turn him away. I believe he is a good guy and that he will be good for you."

"Thanks, girl. I think so too," Paige agreed as the two friends hugged.

"Speaking of Dani, is she in this morning?" Paige inquired.

"She's been in already. She had an early morning appointment with a client, but she should be back in a couple of hours."

Nodding, Paige picked up her messages and continued into her office. Sitting at her desk, her mind returned to Anderson.

"I will give him a real chance," Paige vowed, before digging into her work for the day.

#

Dani stood at the door of her potential client waiting for it to be answered. She was puzzled by this job. The client's assistant made all the arrangements for her to interview at that address, but would not disclose who she worked for. Even upon making the appointment, the assistant stressed to Andee that she was to speak directly to Dani and no one else.

On her drive through the neighborhood, she noted that it was one of the most exclusive in the city. The estates were well maintained and manicured, with everything in its proper place and picture-perfect. Arriving at her destination, Dani took in her surroundings, duly impressed with the grounds. The landscaping could have been pulled from any home and garden show, with its exotic foliage and trees. The mansion itself was large, but not overwhelming. Everything about it was subtle and elegant.

Standing there Dani just hoped that this wasn't some sort of setup and that she would live to regret coming there. She just couldn't figure out why the client was being so secretive.

"Miss Sinclair?" The maid asked Dani when she opened the ornate wooden door.

"Yes, I'm Dani Sinclair," she answered the older woman.

"Come with me please," the woman told Dani, as she stepped aside to allow her to enter. After the maid closed the door she asked Dani to follow her further into the house.

Dani took in her surroundings as she followed the older woman, taking note of the sparsely furnished house. The home itself was beautiful with its grand staircase, highly polished marble floors, and intricate molding detail. Dani was in heaven. Her designer's mind was working a mile a minute, with the possibilities that she saw there. The maid led her into what seemed to be the beginnings of a library, told her to wait there, and left. Dani was so engrossed in the room's potential, that she failed to notice the man who had joined her.

He assessed his guest as she walked around the room. She was as beautiful as he remembered when he first saw her at the charity event. Although he was in attendance, he was not seen by most of the other guests. He had only planned to make a quick appearance, leave a donation, and depart before the press got wind that he was there. He never liked the media's attention, unless it was used to further his business.

He was about to leave when he saw the most beautiful woman he had seen in a long time. She was a dark beauty. The dress she wore was simple, yet it embraced her as if it were a part of her. At five feet ten, she had a body that had curves in all the right places. Yes, she was a woman who made every man in the ballroom that night take notice as she toured the room, chatting with some of the other attending guests. Her slightly exotic features complimented her, as well as her dark, straight, waist-length hair, which was held in place by a diamond-encrusted clamp. Once he saw her, he had to know this woman. After inquiring as to who she was, he placed a call to set in motion, plans to see her again. With this accomplished, he took one last look at her before leaving the ballroom, anticipating their meeting today.

"Ms. Sinclair?" The man finally spoke after observing Dani for a few more moments.

Hearing her name, Dani turned to face the person who spoke it. She was equally in awe. The man who stood before her was beyond handsome. He was over six feet tall, with an athlete's body. His skin the color of a smooth latte was complimented by a head of unruly reddish-brown curls, that begged her to run her fingers through them. The man's eyes were amber brown, with flecks of gold that seemed to sparkle from the room's lighting. His face was clean-shaven except for a neatly trimmed mustache that framed his smiling mouth.

Dani was speechless. "Yes, I'm Dani Sinclair," she managed to breathe out, after a couple of seconds of hesitation.

"Hello Ms. Sinclair, my name is Devin Powers. I would love for you to work your magic and turn this place into a home. Do you think that you could do that for me?" Devin asked in an all too masculine voice that Dani found mesmerizing.

Oh my goodness, she thought. Devin Powers was one of the most powerful African American businessmen in the country and he wanted her to decorate his home. She had read about him and his business ventures, but never really paid that much attention to what was written about the man himself. She knew that he was in his early forties and that he was rated number thirteen in the country in wealth, by the business magazines, but she had no idea what the man looked like until now. She just hoped that she wasn't standing there, with a silly expression on her face.

Not waiting for her answer Devin spoke again. "I hope you weren't too put off by all the cloak-and-dagger tactics that were used to get you here," he was saying. "I value my privacy and want as little attention as possible drawn to myself, as you may be able to understand."

Dani knew from the articles, that she had read regarding him, he was considered almost a recluse because he didn't desire the spotlight as most people in his position did. Devin Powers wasn't a clubber or womanizer, so the tabloids could never catch him at anything newsworthy. By all accounts, Devin Powers was a man of mystery.

Finding her voice again, Dani snapped out of her paralysis and answered him.

"I must admit Mr. Powers, I was a little concerned, but curious all the same. And to answer your first question, without a doubt. I can turn this place into the home of your dreams."

"Well, in that case, you have the job. And please call me Devin."

Chapter 18

After becoming a couple, Paige and Anderson spent all their free time together, learning and enjoying each other. They discovered they had quite a few things in common. They both enjoyed visiting various museums and often drove to nearby cities to attend art exhibits and fundraisers. They often patronized unconventional eateries, to try new and exotic foods, that gave Anderson ideas for his own, personal concoctions.

That evening, they were enjoying dinner at a newly opened restaurant, that boasted of its authentic Cantonese cuisine, in a nearby town. They had spent the day driving around the small scenic city, browsing flea markets, antique shops, and yard sales; just enjoying each other's company.

During dinner, they discovered they both shared a love for sun, sand, and surf, along with their shared love for antiquing. They even discussed plans for a future tropical getaway together. The more time Paige spent with Anderson, the deeper her feelings grew for him. He made her feel alive. Anderson had awakened in her the desire to give him what he asked—all of her.

They were just finishing their meal, when an impeccably dressed older gentleman, accompanied by a young woman, stopped abruptly while passing their table. His sudden actions drew both Paige's and Anderson's attention.

"Anderson?...son?" The man asked in a voice of wonder.

Paige saw the resemblance immediately. The man had to be Anderson's father, and after giving the young woman a closer examination, she knew she was his sister. They both bore this man's remarkable features, although Paige could also glimpse the young woman's Spanish heritage.

Paige watched Anderson drop his napkin onto the table and slowly stand to his feet, staring eye-to-eye with the man. For a quick second, she saw fear in the older man's eyes. It was so brief, that she began to believe she had imagined it. The man took a slight step back, as she and the younger woman divided their attention between Anderson and his father. Paige watched, as a myriad of emotions played across Anderson's face. She held her breath, waiting to see which one would win out.

After staring at the man, for what seemed like ages, Anderson finally spoke.

"I'm not your son old man. You gave up the right to call me that the day you left me and your pregnant wife to fend for ourselves."

In his response to his father, Anderson caught movement out of the corner of his eye. The young woman who stood next to her father stepped closer.

Seeing the girl for the first time, Anderson studied her, realizing that indeed, she was his sister. He looked back at the man who gave him life and spoke again, not to his father, but to his sister.

"I'm sorry we had to meet under these circumstances little Sis, but knowing who this man is, I'm sure he didn't bother to tell you about the family he voluntarily gave up, to start a whole new one," Anderson spoke to her with deadly calm.

The girl looked at her father, and then her brother. "Anderson, my name is Mia and yes I am your sister, but you're wrong about our father. He's told me about you and Jayden. Anderson, papa is very sorry for what he's done. Can you find it in your heart to forgive him?" She pleaded with him.

Anderson's jaw tightened, as he stood staring at his father. Here stood this well-to-do and well-dressed man, not looking much older than he did the day he left;

certainly not much worse for wear. Anderson thought of all the sacrifices, that his mother had to make, to ensure he and his brother had shelter and food. Here his father stood looking as if he never missed a beat.

Removing his wallet from his pocket, Anderson dropped more than enough money for their meal and tip onto the table.

Finally returning his gaze to Mia, he answered her. "You may be able to forgive him, but I can't. He didn't leave you."

"Come on Paige we're leaving." With that said, Paige rose to join him; leaving the pair standing there.

Anderson's father watched with unshed tears in his eyes.

#

Remembering how Anderson gave her space, after her confrontation with Jean, Paige let him have his quiet time on the drive back to his house. From the little that she witnessed, Paige gathered that the senior Stone had left his family, creating a terrible time for Anderson. This explained why he didn't want to talk about his father. She couldn't much blame him, but she still was curious to know the full story.

Pulling into his driveway, Anderson killed the engine and stared into space. Without a preamble, he began the tale of his father.

"I was about six years old. I was walking home from school that day when I spotted my father's truck parked in the driveway. I ran the rest of the way because I was so excited that Daddy was home. You see, my father worked for one of the big rail companies, and his job took him all over the country on those trains, which meant he wasn't home much." Anderson shook his head slowly, remembering as if it were yesterday.

"When dad was home it was fun times," he continued with a small smile. "Mom would always cook a big dinner of his favorite foods. He would always have some sort of gift for us. We would have movie night or go to an amusement park…it didn't matter as long as we were all together."

"As soon as I entered the house that day, I knew something was wrong. There was no food cooking, no gifts sitting on the dining table. I heard my father's voice and it didn't sound right, so I didn't go into their bedroom. I stood just inside the kitchen doorway where I could hear but not be seen. I heard him tell my mother that he was leaving because he couldn't handle family life…he couldn't be her husband or my father anymore."

Anderson paused, struggling to get his emotions under control. Paige touched his arm then, trying to give him some sort of comfort, letting him know she was there for him. She felt terrible for him.

Finally able to continue, Anderson closed his eyes, swallowed, and pressed on. "I heard my mother ask him why. How could he just come home and drop a bomb like that and just leave? She was on the edge of hysteria. She just kept asking him why?"

He looked at Paige then, but she didn't think that he saw her. He was back in a time that she could never see, a time that only he could experience.

"He never really answered her," he continued, shaking his head. "He just packed that duffle bag he always carried, and left. He left my pregnant mother standing there crying and never looked back."

Anderson sighed heavily. He looked so weary sitting there reliving that painful time in his life.

Paige finally understood why he reacted the way he did to his father, and why he reacted to her questions about him. She suspected, that he had been holding that hurt inside of himself all of this time, never releasing it. She knew she would be there for him when he finally let it all out, letting go of it for good. He had to let go of it for him to heal.

She and Anderson finally made their way inside the house. They had talked well into the night about his family, his father. She asks questions with him giving answers. Paige learned that Anderson's mother, Adaisha, had to go back into the workforce after over eight years of being a housewife. She had no choice. She had a child to care for and another one on the way.

He told her about having to leave their big comfortable home and move to a small cramped one. Anderson had watched his mother go from a happy woman to a tired and drawn one, always working long hours to keep their heads above water.

When Jayden was born, he helped his mother care for him. There were times when he would change Jayden's diapers, feed him, and play with him, so his mother could get some much-needed rest. Paige could tell that his talking aloud about his life and his father, seemed to lift a weight off of him. She realized that he had never shared this part of himself with anyone. His mother didn't even know how he felt.

"After I'd gotten my first high-paying position as a licensed attorney, and Jayden was well established on his job, we pooled our money together and bought our mother a lovely home in a gated community. She'd worked so hard to raise us and deserves to be treated well after what Rendell put her through," he told her with much feeling. "Our mother deserves all the comforts and luxuries that we can give her." For the first time that night, Anderson smiled. The thought of his mother always brought him peace.

#

Paige woke up the next morning replaying the events of the night before. She thought about how Rendell's actions had molded Anderson into the man that he is today. She reflected on how giving and loving he was. A stark contrast to who his father was. She couldn't imagine what it was like to have a parent selfishly walk away from his family. She shook her head. She felt sorry for Rendell because he missed out on watching Anderson grow into a wonderfully strong man.

Sighing, she got out of bed to start her day. She hated having to leave Anderson, after all that he had experienced that night, but she had a very early morning appointment that she needed to prepare for. So he had driven her back to her house, promising to pick her up after work for a quiet, relaxing evening

Chapter 19

After spending another great evening with Anderson, Paige arrived at *Beautiful Colors* feeling as if she had won the lottery. She and Anderson had spent the rainy night together at his home, just enjoying each other's company. They had made a pact not to mention his father or anything about him. Anderson just wanted to concentrate solely on Paige.

As always, Anderson was the perfect gentleman, even though she could feel he wanted to take their relationship to the next level. He pledged that he would wait for her until she was sure that their relationship was solid and he kept his word. She had grown to trust him, believing that he meant every word that he said.

Arriving at the reception area, Paige nodded to Andee who was busy working the phones. Collecting her messages she proceeded on into her office. Sitting at her desk, she found it difficult to concentrate, with Anderson's handsome face continuously appearing in her mind.

Soon she thought. Very soon I will give you what we both want. With that decision made, she picked up the phone to place an order with one of their vendors.

#

Sitting at his desk across town, Anderson was finding it hard to concentrate on his work. He sat in his office, facing the wall of windows that overlooked the river. Barges and ships moved along on the water, but he didn't notice, because his mind was too filled with Paige.

Anderson found her to be an incredible woman, although he didn't think that she was conscious of that fact. She seemed to be unaware of the effect she had on him, hell on men in general. She didn't see how his pulse raced at the mere sight of her or when they kissed, how he wanted to lose control, making it almost impossible for him to walk away without loving her. For Anderson, just being near Paige made the rest of the world fall away, leaving only them. She was so beautiful. Sitting there looking out of the window, he realized that he was falling in love and he didn't want to stop.

"Anderson...."

His assistant's voice came over the intercom hesitantly. She paused not knowing how to continue.

"Yes, Taylor...?" Anderson answered puzzled by her behavior.

Trying again, Taylor pressed forward.

"There is a woman on the phone who says that she's your sister, Mia?"

Anderson sat up in his chair. Mia, he had forgotten about her. He had been so focused on his bastard of a father, that he had completely forgotten about Mia. He was not prepared to deal with her at the moment, so he asked Taylor to take a message and explain that he was in a meeting and would call her back. He also promised to explain to Taylor, his cousin from his mother's side of the family, what was going on later.

Anderson knew that he would have to deal with this situation eventually, he just preferred to deal with it later rather than sooner. His sister, he and Jayden had a sister. Thinking of Jayden, Anderson groaned. He would have to tell Jayden about his run-in with their father after all these years. He wondered how he would take it. Jayden never had the opportunity to meet the man. Rendell was long gone before Jayden was born. However his brother reacted, he knew they both must protect their mother at all costs. Anderson didn't want Adaisha to find out about Rendell's other family. She was happy now and he didn't want anything to change that. He made a mental note to contact his brother soon before Mia or Rendell got to him.

Taylor buzzed in again, bringing him out of his reverie. "Anderson, your appointment is here."

"Send him in Taylor." Pulling his mind back to the business at hand, Anderson stood to greet his appointment.

Justin Graham strolled into the room, making his way to where Anderson was waiting. Anderson didn't know much about this potential client because it was a last-minute appointment Taylor had set up just that morning. He was aware it was a divorce involving a growing corporation but that was the only information he had received. He usually did not meet with clients without doing some background work to determine if a meeting would be necessary, but something in his gut told him that he should meet with this one.

"Good morning Mr. Stone," Justin greeted, extending his hand. "My name is Justin Graham and I need your help."

Mentally, Anderson raised an eyebrow upon hearing the man's name. *So this is the idiot that hurt Paige.*

Although surprised, he gave no outward appearance of any kind, that he was aware of who Justin was. Anderson accepted the man's handshake and motioned for him to sit.

He knew the moment Justin introduced himself, that he wouldn't be taking his case no matter what it was. Anderson sat there sizing him up, as Justin explained he was in the middle of a divorce and wanted to know what his options were for his business. Anderson wondered what the man was really up to. Justin claimed that he was in the process of opening a second office in another state and his divorce attorney suggested he talk to someone in corporate law on how to proceed. Anderson was quite sure the man wasn't telling the truth. Any attorney, including his divorce attorney, could have given him that information. Anderson wondered if Justin knew he was seeing Paige. If so, was he there to check out the competition, while considering his options with her?

After letting Justin lay out his purpose for being there, Anderson stood and informed him, that he would have to look into the matter further, to determine if he had the time to give the case the proper attention that it deserved. Again shaking hands, Anderson watched Justin leave his office. The man was up to something, Anderson was sure of it. As soon as he was certain Justin had left, he buzzed Taylor and told her to send him a letter of regret, that he would not be taking his case. Anderson rocked in his chair disturbed. He had a feeling that he hadn't seen the last of Justin Graham.

Chapter 20

Dani didn't bother to go into the office. She called Andee earlier and told her that she was working on a client's home and would be out for the day. She was glad that Andee was too preoccupied with her infatuation with Jayden, to notice that she was being secretive. She chuckled at having teased her about keeping secrets concerning her romance because she had a few secrets of her own. One was, that she was very attracted to her new client and she wouldn't mind one bit if, after the job, there could be more than a work-related relationship between them. Given half a chance, she would certainly do something about that attraction.

After she agreed to decorate Devin Powers' home, he gave her one condition upon doing so. She had to remain mum as to whose house she was working on. Although she didn't fully understand why, she agreed to his terms. He explained to her that no one else could know, not even her crew. Devin made it clear that, whenever the crew worked in the house he would not be present.

Her crew didn't start for another couple of days so she was sure that they would be alone today, while she went over some of the colors and fabrics that she had chosen. He also made it clear that he wanted to be a part of the process. Normally that did not bother her, but with Devin, it was going to be a little difficult to focus on her work, because of her attraction. She felt the pull the moment he spoke her name.

"What have I gotten myself into?" Dani muttered with a shake of her head, as she pulled to a stop in Devin's circular driveway.

Getting out of the car with her briefcase and sample case, she walked on nervous legs to the door. She was just about to ring the bell when the door opened. Expecting to see the maid, Dani was surprised when Devin stood before her.

"Ms. Sinclair, you're right on time. I like that." Devin complimented her punctuality with a grin.

"Call me Dani please and yes I believe in being professional at all times," she threw back with a smile of her own.

"Come in." Devin stepped aside to allow her to enter. "You can take your things into the library and I will join you there in a moment."

When she passed him, Devin was able to get a glance of her firm and full breasts, encased in a sleeveless silver button-down blouse. Her hair was swept back into a long ponytail held together with that diamond-encrusted clamp he noticed at the banquet. Devin longed to release that clamp and let her hair flow around her bare shoulders and back.

The next thing that grabbed his attention was her shapely legs, accentuated by the four-inch navy pumps that she wore. His eyes admired the navy blue high-waisted skirt that stopped mid-thigh. Devin then let his eyes travel to her rounded hips, which swayed with every step that she took.

Reaching the library, Dani was very aware that Devin had all but undressed her with his eyes. *So he likes what he sees*, she thought smiling to herself. *Yes, this will be a very interesting job indeed*, she mused as she began her task. She placed fabric and color samples on a nearby table all the while making some mental notes as to what colors should go where. She would leave samples in each room as she and Devin toured the house saving her time and mistakes.

"Would you like to get started now?" Devin asked Dani when he entered the room.

"Yes, where shall we start?" Dani asked.

"Well, let's start upstairs and work our way down."

Dani gathered her materials and followed Devin upstairs. When they reached the second level, they discussed color schemes to be used for the walls, windows, and floor. Devin chose the carpet, wallpaper, and paint colors that he wanted to use in each area. Moving from room to room, the process went smoothly, with Dani making notes and leaving samples of the materials to be used. When they reached Devin's master suite, the only thing that graced the room was a huge four-poster bed.

"Is this the only piece of furniture you have for this room?" Dani asked surprised.

In each of the other rooms they visited, there was an ample amount of furniture, but when it came to this room it was bare except for the huge bed.

"Yes at the moment this is all that I have. I was hoping we could start in here," Devin suggested.

He watched her expression change from surprised, to puzzled, to resigned. He believed the more challenges he gave her, the more time he would have to observe her. He was determined to know everything about her and for him, that meant consuming most of her time.

"Ok…I don't usually start this way, but…I guess we can start here." Dani was perplexed.

"Good! But first I think that we should get something out of the way before we go any further," Devin said, walking towards her.

"What is—"

Before Dani could finish her sentence, she found herself in Devin's arms being thoroughly kissed.

He kissed her so quickly, that she didn't have time to protest, even if she wanted to and she didn't want to. Devin, feeling no resistance from her, deepened the kiss, while pulling her more firmly into his arms. He hadn't meant to kiss her, but looking at her standing there, in his home, in his bedroom, he couldn't help himself. He prolonged the kiss as long as he could, to convey the message that he wanted Dani to receive. He meant to have her, and not just for a while, but for always.

"Do you always kiss women that you barely know Devin?" Dani asked after they both had to come up for air. She was still reeling from that incredible kiss, as well as the feelings that came along with it.

"No Dani that was reserved only for you. You have to know by now, that I am very much attracted to you. I couldn't help myself. Also, if I'm not mistaken, from the way you responded, the feeling is mutual."

"Yes Devin, the feeling is mutual," Dani admitted. "So tell me. What shall we do about these...feelings?" She asked him with a wicked grin.

"Do you really want to know what I think we should do about these feelings?" Devin asked.

"Yes, I do," Dani answered him still smiling, but not knowing what to expect from this man.

She watched as Devin's hands moved to her blouse. Slowly, one by one he released each button. After this task was completed, he removed the blouse from her body, all the while kissing her mouth, and her neck. Dani moaned with anticipation. Tossing the blouse to the floor, Devin reached behind her, to slide the zipper down to release her from her skirt. She stared into Devin's eyes watching them turn dark with passion, making her tremble. Once the skirt hit the floor, he took a step back to admire her body.

"Beautiful," was all that Devin could utter.

He watched her step out of the skirt, which pooled at her feet. Dani stood before him, clad only in her navy blue bra, panties, and pumps. Something is needed here he thought, as his gaze traveled over her beautiful body. Realizing what it was he needed to see, Devin stepped closer to release her hair that was held captive by the clamp. He watched as it flowed around her shoulders and across her back.

"I've wanted to do that since the first time I saw you," Devin whispered.

Dani stood there in her underwear amused. She had never been ashamed of her body and to have this sexy man admiring it made her bold.

"So now what?" She asked, wondering what he would do next.

Devin answered, by picking her up and carrying her to his bed. He laid her in its middle as if she were something delicate, something that needed to be cherished. Dani watched him hurriedly remove his clothing. The man's body was simply gorgeous. She let her eyes roam his abs, his pecs, his thighs. He was divine.

Devin joined her on the bed, covering her with his body. He took his time as if he had all the time in the world. He kissed her, while his hands traveled over her well-toned form. He kissed the tops of her full breasts, which threatened to spill from her bra. He kissed her neck, her mouth. Dani was enraptured by this man. She couldn't think straight. He wouldn't allow her to, with the things he was doing to her body, to her mind.

"I want you, Dani," Devin hoarsely whispered. "Say that you will be mine." Devin pleaded.

"Yes, I want you too," Dani answered him breathlessly.

Devin didn't think she understood what he was asking of her. He wanted her, not just as his lover, but as his wife. He would not have ever thought, that love at first sight existed. But when he saw her, he knew it could be true. He would have to make her understand later. But for now, he had to obey his body's command to love her.

Devin moved away from Dani to remove her panties and bra, the last barriers that separated them. After he removed her lingerie, Dani attempted to remove her pumps, but he stopped her.

"No, leave them. I want to see you in them while we make love." He then proceeded, to kiss her stomach, her breasts, her mouth, as he caressed her hair.

While Devin explored her body, Dani's fingers were firmly entwined in his thick curls. Curls, she had longed to touch from the beginning. When the heat between them had risen beyond control, she had to resist pulling them.

Dani moaned, moving wildly, when he progressed farther south, to worship at her alter. She didn't know that she could feel this wanted, this loved. This last thought confused her. However, she was unable to fully explore it at the moment, so she filed it away for later.

Not being able to hold off any longer, Devin moved away from his love, only long enough for him to apply protection. Moving back to her, he took her with one powerful thrust. Devin thought he would lose his mind from the pleasure he felt. Joining with her was like finding his other half. The half he had searched for his entire life. He had always gotten high from his business acquisitions, but this was beyond any high he could have ever imagined. He began to move after recovering from the shock of joining his body with the woman he would marry. Loving her always.

He observed Dani as he thrust deeper. Taking his time with each stroke. She matched him move for move as if she knew his body better than he did himself. She hung on to him, never taking her eyes from his. He could tell she was searching. Searching for what made her feel the way she did. He knew she was experiencing the same feelings he felt. Although she found it exciting, he could tell that it was also a little frightening for her. All in all, she never stopped and never missed a stroke. He knew she would try to sort it all out later.

Chapter 21

Paige was just finishing a long day when her mobile phone rang. It was Anderson.

Smiling, she answered. "Hi, Anderson. How has your day been?" She asked.

"It's been... interesting. I was wondering if you were free for dinner tonight, so I can tell you all about it. There's this Thai restaurant that I want to try so can we discuss it then?."

"Thai, that sounds good to me," Paige responded.

"Ok lady, I will pick you up by 6:30. See you then."

Still smiling, Paige clicked off and prepared to leave. But before she could, her phone rang again. Thinking that it was Anderson calling back, she quickly answered.

"What did you forget?" She asked in a sultry voice.

"Hello, Paige, it's Justin."

Paige's smile quickly turned into a frown. Justin? why was he calling her? When he left her that night he finished breaking her heart, she didn't expect to ever hear from him again, at least that was what he led her to believe, and she had counted just on that. He said he swore he would leave her alone to live her life, to be happy with someone else. She had found that someone in Anderson. So why was he calling now?

"Justin, why are you calling?" She asked him, annoyed.

"I know that I said I wouldn't, but I wanted you to know that I'm getting a divorce. Paige, baby, I still love you. I would like to see you once the divorce is finalized," Justin explained.

Paige held the phone away from her, staring at it, as if it had suddenly come to life. *He must be kidding,* she thought. *Why did he think that he could walk in and out of her life, whenever he got good and damn ready?*

This intrusion verified that what she thought she knew of Justin was never true. She could finally see him for the selfish bastard he truly was. At this moment Paige's heart grew indifferent to him. She wanted nothing more to do with Justin Graham.

"Paige, are you still there?" Justin asked, thinking she had ended the call.

"I'm here," Paige answered. "Justin, you and I have nothing more to say to each other. I would appreciate it if you would not contact me again," She added, before disconnecting the call, hopefully for the final time.

Paige sat at her desk, thinking about what just happened. She couldn't believe he could be so selfish. Just when she had gotten past everything he had done, he resurfaced again. He was determined to try to wreak more havoc in her life. The more she thought about it, the more annoyed she became.

He has some nerve, she thought, shaking her head in dismay. At that moment, Paige knew she was over Justin. All she could see was Anderson's smiling face.

Smiling again, she grabbed her purse and headed for the door. She had to head home, to get ready for her date with Anderson.

Chapter 22

Justin was furious.

"How dare she hang up on me!" He couldn't believe Paige had dismissed him so callously.

Slamming the phone onto his desk, he bound from his chair to pace his office. Ever since he saw Paige with Stone, at that banquet, he knew he couldn't just let her go. There she was laughing and talking with Stone. She was supposed to have eyes for him, not that jerk.

Justin had kept close tabs on Paige, over the past months. He was glad to see, that she wasn't seeing anyone. He thought if he gave her some time, she would miss him to the point, that it wouldn't matter that he was married. He knew she still had feelings for him. He would have everything he wanted, a prestigious wife, a successful business, and Paige, his Paige. But she had met Anderson Stone.

"Damn it!" Justin stopped pacing to pound on his desk.

#

Justin had attended the gala to "accidentally" run into Paige. He wanted to try and feel her out, as to how he could get back into her life. He knew she had to be lonely.

She would need someone, need him. But, Stone was there before he could maneuver himself into position to talk to her.

He watched them dance. He watched that cow Jean say something to upset Paige, sending her practically running from the dance floor. He was just about to follow her to the ladies' room when he was stopped short by Anderson's presence.

Justin watched Anderson take Paige's hand, leading her from the hotel. At that point, he wasn't quite sure, what was happening between them. That was until he followed them to Paige's home.

Justin sat across the street in his car waiting. He waited for Anderson to leave, to talk to Paige. With each passing moment, Justin couldn't stand not knowing what was going on inside. With his mind racing he left his car to see for himself. Hidden from street view, by shrubbery that surrounded the front of her house, he peered into Paige's living room window. What he saw stunned him. Anderson was kissing Paige. Justin rushed back to his car enraged.

Justin cursed Anastasia the entire drive to his place. If she hadn't gotten pregnant, he and Paige would still been together. He chose to overlook his willingness to sleep with Anastasia. He considered that as the cost of doing business.

Anastasia had implied, she would give him a lucrative contract with her family's companies, if he did so. He just didn't consider she may have had a plan of her own.

Anastasia wanted Justin as her husband, and she was willing to make that happen whatever the cost. Unfortunately for Justin, he had no choice once the baby was involved. He knew Anastasia would make good on her threats to ruin him. That much of the story he told Paige was true he just didn't tell her the whole truth.

#

Justin met Anastasia on the first day of the retreat. He sought her out. Justin knew, that if he could get her family's business to sign with him, most of the other prominent companies would follow suit. He wined and dined Anastasia for the next two nights, trying to persuade her to sign with his firm.

Anastasia was enamored with Justin and agreed to give him a signed contract if he would have dinner with her in her suite. Justin had greedily agreed to her terms and joined her on the last night of the retreat. He knew what she wanted, and he was prepared to deliver. He would do almost anything to seal the deal.

He met Anastasia in her suite that night as required. Though they did have dinner, Justin willingly found himself in bed as Anastasia's dessert. She was a beautiful, desirable woman, which made the task a piece of cake.

After spending a few hours with her, giving in to her desires, Justin left with the signed contracts in hand. He was a happy man or so he thought. When he got back to his suite, he realized what he had done, but comforted himself with scotch and the reassurance that what had just taken place was for the good of his company. He convinced himself that business deals were made that way every day.

Even with the internal pep talk, Justin still felt a bit uneasy, so he called Paige to ease his conscience and reassure himself that all was right within his world. After hearing Paige's soothing voice, he pushed the incident out of his mind and left it at that. But Anastasia had to let herself get pregnant, leaving him no choice but to marry her, taking him away from Paige, his Paige.

After witnessing the spectacle between Paige and Anderson, Justin needed a plan. So he decided to visit Stone to see what he was up against. However, after meeting Anderson, Justin left puzzled. It appeared Anderson knew nothing of him or his connection to Paige. Justin didn't know what to make of that. Why hadn't she shared their relationship with this new man? What did this mean for him? Had Paige gotten over him and moved on? He didn't think so.

"I will get you back Paige…yes I will," Justin vowed.

Chapter 23

"Anderson, what's the matter? You were unusually quiet during dinner tonight."

Paige sat curled up next to him concerned. He seemed to have been deep in thought all night. They had come back to his house to continue their date.

"I had an interesting visitor today," Anderson started. "I just don't know what to make of it. On the surface, it seemed to have been just another consult. Although, the more that I think about it," he added shaking his head, "I believe that it was a fishing expedition," he finished with a resigned sigh.

Hearing the strain in his voice, Paige immediately sat up, alarmed. "Tell me."

Anderson sighed again heavily. Drawing his hand down his face, before he spoke.

"Justin Graham came to see me today. He claimed that he was seeking some information. Information, on how to proceed with his business. He also claimed that he was in the middle of a divorce."

"But Paige...it just doesn't add up. His own attorney could have given him that information. I believe he knows you and I are seeing each other, and his little visit was to see who he was up against," Anderson concluded.

"I think you have a right to be suspicious. He called me right before I left the office, mentioning that he was getting a divorce and wanted back into my life."

Anderson stared at Paige troubled. Wondering what that meant for them. Did she want Justin back? Will this be the end of their relationship? He couldn't lose her, not now. He loved her.

He opened his mouth to voice his fears, but Paige spoke before he could ask those heart-wrenching questions.

"Anderson," she began, cradling his face in her hands. "You don't have to worry about Justin. He is not a threat to us. I was done with him the moment he revealed he married Anastasia." She leaned in and kissed him. Trying to reassure him that he had nothing to worry about.

"Baby, are you sure? I don't want to lose you," he confessed, needing to believe her.

"Anderson, you have all of me. You don't have to worry about him or any other man for that matter. I love you and only you."

Paige professed her love with joyful tears. Yes, she loved him. She loved him in a way she never loved Justin. In a way, she would never love any other man.

Anderson gazed into her eyes, finally seeing what he had been waiting for. She looked at him as if witnessing the depths of forever. He knew then, that she truly had given him all of herself.

Well not quite, he thought with a grin. He would soon take care of that.

Anderson kissed her then. Possessing her with his mouth. He felt himself grow and harden, as his hands wandered over her body. He had been waiting so long for this moment, and now it had come.

Lifting Paige, he sat her on his lap to gain better access to her mouth and body. He moaned when her bottom came in contact with his growing erection.

"I love you so much Paige, so much," he whispered, staring into her eyes, before he kissed her again.

He ran his hand up her thigh, under her skirt, to find the treasure that he was seeking. Finding it, he pressed his palm there, causing her to moan her approval. She was so wet, so soft. Sensing that she was ready for him, Anderson carried her to his bedroom, to his bed. The same bed they both had fantasized about.

After placing Paige in the bed's center, he undressed her and then himself. Never letting his gaze leave her. With this task completed, he joined her there, kissing his way to his goal, starting with her toes. He kissed each one. Sucking them into his mouth, savoring the reaction he drew from her. Moving farther up, he lifted each leg in turn. Kissing each calf. Running his tongue softly up her calves to the back of her knees and thighs.

From there he moved to her inner thighs, all the while Paige was going out of her mind with pleasure. She called his name repeatedly as if it were the only word she knew. As he made his way to his destination, he placed her legs over his shoulders, delving deep with his tongue. Paige thought she would lose it, from the erotic sensations that he produced within her. Her body, moving with his mouth at a feverish pace, threatened to break apart. She had never felt pleasure like this. She couldn't think. She couldn't speak. All she could do was feel, and the feeling was awesome.

Anderson let Paige climax over his tongue before he moved away to protect them. She watched him slowly roll the condom onto his full erection. He was enormous. She began to have doubts. Fearing that her body wouldn't accommodate him.

Aware of her apprehension, Anderson quickly assured her, that he would take his time and not hurt her.

Moving back to her, he slowly massaged her inner thighs with the pads of his thumbs; paying detailed attention to the area close to her gem. Anderson eased her fears with each stroke of his powerful hands. When he felt she was ready, he eased inside of her, taking his time with each thrust. She closed around him tightly, nearly taking his breath away. He stilled himself. Clenching his teeth. Fighting for control, and afraid that he would lose it. As her body adjusted to him, Anderson began to thrust deeper, until all of him was inside of her.

He found his rhythm then, loving the way she felt. Even in the best of fantasies, he could not have imagined this taste of heaven. As she began to move with him, Anderson picked up the tempo, moving faster, deeper; observing Paige's reaction to him with each stroke. She was lost in him, moving with him as if they were one being. They both cried out with pleasure. Riding the wave, which was their love for each other. Feeling her body tighten even more around him, Anderson heightened the tempo, riding the wave even more, bringing her with him. Paige hung on until she couldn't. Finally letting go with a scream of his name. Anderson came with her, with a force never known before. They both let go, riding that last wave until they floated gently back to shore.

Anderson, breathing heavily, gathered Paige into his arms kissing her, telling her how much he loved her. He couldn't believe how incredible their joining had been. He would love this woman for eternity, and no one would come between them. He had only taken a few minutes for reflection before he rolled over and mounted her again. This, he repeated all during the night, with Paige right there with him at every stroke.

\#

At Devin's, Dani came awake with a start. Where was she? She asked herself, trying to remember. Then it all came back to her.

"Oh my goodness, what have I done?" She whispered.

Even though the room was dark, she could see that Devin was asleep beside her. She saw his silhouette, by way of the moonlight, shining through the uncovered window.

Easing out of bed, she gathered her things and hurried downstairs, where she dressed and made her way to her car. Sitting behind the wheel, Dani couldn't believe she slept with a client. This was so unprofessional. What must Devin think of her?

"Devin, oh God, Devin." She began to cry, although she didn't understand why.

Suddenly, she realized she needed to leave before he woke up. With the thought of Devin confronting her for sneaking out, Dani started the car and drove off.

Hearing Dani's car start through the open window, Devin came awake reaching for her. Not finding her next to him, he realized she had left. He sat up stretching, remembering what he and Dani had shared. It was incredible.

Although he was disappointed, he understood why she left. She was confused. Experiencing emotions, she didn't understand. He understood he would make her understand. He would let her go, for now, but when he came for her, he wouldn't let her go again.

Chapter 24

Paige woke right before dawn. Anderson was sound asleep. After the way he loved her all during the night, she knew he was exhausted. Smiling, she studied while he slept. The man was beautiful even then. She smoothed his brow, loving what she saw. She loved this man. This man, whom she tried hard not to love. How could she think that she ever fully loved Justin? He couldn't begin to match what she was feeling for Anderson. Paige couldn't imagine living without him. Yes, he had all of her and he always would.

Anderson stirred opening his eyes. He smiled up at a still-smiling Paige. He felt she was right where she should be, in his bed. Bringing her closer he kissed her.

"Good morning baby."

"I love you." She said kissing him back.

"Now that's what I like to hear first thing in the morning," Anderson replied. He turned onto his back and pulled her on top of him.

Laughing, Paige asked, "Do you ever get enough?" Indicating his erection, that lay between them.

"Not when it comes to you, my love."

Reaching into the nightstand, he took out a condom and handed it to her. Paige sat up and slowly rolled it onto the evidence of his love for her. With this done, he lifted her and placed her firmly, unto what was solely hers.

She began to move, rocking back and forth, slowly at first. But as the heat grew between them, she rode him wildly, unable to control herself. With her every movement, Anderson thrust upward, meeting her time after time. Unable to wait any longer, he flipped her over onto her back. Still coupled together, he took control. Thrusting deeper, faster, until they came as one.

Gathered in each other's arms, they whispered words of endearment, until they both fell back to sleep. Both were secure in their love for each other.

#

"Anderson this is so good. I didn't realize how hungry I was." Paige was enjoying the meal Anderson prepared.

Kissing her as he poured her more coffee. "I'm glad you're enjoying it. We did work up quite an appetite," he playfully added, kissing her again.

Anderson had prepared a feast of a breakfast. There was bacon, fluffy scrambled eggs, waffles topped with strawberries, grits, and hash browns, all of Paige's favorites.

They slept later than they had planned, so technically the meal was lunch instead of breakfast. Neither of them noticed, or cared, as long as they were with each other. They planned to venture out later, to do some shopping and catch a movie, but at that moment, they were content in just being with each other, loving each other.

Chapter 25

Justin was beside himself. He had waited outside of Paige's house most of the night. Waiting for her to come home, but she never did. He had parked across from Paige's the night before, just as Anderson arrived to pick her up, on what he assumed was just a date. He had waited for hours for them to return; wondering where she was.

Did she go to his place? After she didn't return home, he was sure of it. He knew he should have gotten Anderson's address. He had to know what was going on between them. Finally leaving to go home, Justin drove slowly from Paige's neighborhood, trying to decide what to do next.

#

After spending the afternoon watching a movie at the Cineplex, Anderson and Paige decided to do some shopping. Walking hand in hand, they visited some of Paige's favorite stores, with Anderson buying her whatever her heart desired. He loved spoiling her, even though she chose more things for him, instead of herself.

They were browsing resort wear when Paige spotted Jean heading in their direction. Sensing her tension, Anderson was about to ask what was wrong, when Jean reached them. Squeezing Paige's hand, Anderson readied himself to do battle with the awful woman.

"Hi," Jean spoke to them, appearing very uncomfortable.

Neither responded. They waited to see what the woman had in store for them this time.

"Paige, I saw you here in the store and...well, I just wanted to apologize for my behavior the last time I saw you. And what's more, all the other times that I have been unkind to you. I don't know what gets into me sometimes," Jean mumbled with downcast eyes.

After a brief pause, she looked up at them again and continued. "I realized that I have been quite mean to you and that you didn't deserve it. You have never done anything to me. You have even tried to be nice to me. Well...anyway, like I said, I just wanted to say that I'm sorry. I hope that someday you can find it in your heart to forgive me," she ended with hope in her voice.

With that said, and without waiting for a reaction from either of them, Jean simply nodded and walked away.

Paige and Anderson exchanged glances in amazement.

"Well, wonders never cease," Paige stated surprised.

"I wondered what brought that on. Do you think that she was sincere?" Anderson asked.

"I hope so. Although only time will tell," Paige surmised, turning back to the racks of clothes. "Only time will tell," she repeated.

After their encounter with Jean, Anderson suggested they take a vacation, sooner rather than later. He wanted Paige to relax. Especially after she admitted she hadn't taken a vacation in over two years.

With Paige's agreement, they visited a travel agency located there in the mall, before she changed her mind. Once reaching the agency, the couple was so engrossed in travel plans and brochures, that they didn't notice they were being watched.

#

Justin had followed them from Paige's house to the mall. He had gotten back just in time, to see the two arrive back at her home. It was late afternoon, and he could only imagine what they had been doing all night and most of the day, since Paige was wearing the same clothes she had on the night before.

With this new development, Justin angrily gripped the steering wheel. Becoming more irritated, as he observed Anderson kissing Paige, as he helped her from his car.

He watched him place a possessive arm around Paige's waist. He watched them enter the house. He watched seething when Anderson closed the door behind them. Firmly disconnecting his view. Justin sat impatiently waiting for Anderson to leave, hoping he would have a chance to talk to Paige alone. Justin knew he needed to see her sooner, rather than later, before she got too cozy with Anderson Stone.

After waiting nearly an hour, Justin watched in frustration when Anderson exited the house with a laughing Paige in tow, carrying a travel bag. To add to his frustration, he noticed that Paige was genuinely happy. She looked at Anderson as if he were the light of her world.

"She used to look at me like that," Justin said, pounding the armrest. "And she will look at me that way again. She doesn't love him, she still loves me," he told himself.

He pulled away from the curb, to follow them.

#

After booking their vacation, Anderson brought Paige back to his house. They enjoyed a light dinner, after which Paige took a hot shower, and retired to Anderson's bed exhausted. Intending to watch one of her favorite television shows, she fell asleep before the opening credits.

After checking on her, Anderson found Paige asleep. He knew she was tired. He had kept her up most of the night loving her.

Later, Anderson settled himself within the quiet of his media room. The past two days had been perfect, but there was one task he had been avoiding—Rendell. He had exhausted all of the excuses for not dealing with the subject of his father. Anderson groaned. With all of his wishes concerning Paige coming true, it was time to face the unpopular task of informing his brother about their father.

"I may as well get this over with," Anderson mumbled while calling Jayden's number. He had put this on hold long enough.

#

Jayden answered the phone in a good mood, but when Anderson ended their conversation, he was stoic. He didn't know what to make of it. Jayden asked a few questions seemingly detached from the situation.

Anderson didn't know what to expect, but he could somewhat see Jayden's point of view. He had never met the man. The only information he knew, was that told to him by Anderson and their mother. The only thing that he seemed to care about was their newfound sister, Mia. He told Anderson that it was kind of cool to have a little sister and had expressed the fact that he wanted to meet her. Before ending their conversation, they both agreed, that their mother was not to know about anything involving Rendell.

"One call down, one to go," Anderson said this, as he dialed Mia's number.

Chapter 26

Early Monday morning, Dani hid out in her office, still horrified over what she had done with Devin.

"He's a client. Well, he was a client," she lamented with her face in her hands.

She was pretty sure, after her behavior, he wouldn't want her to decorate his house or anything else for that matter. How could she have done something so stupid, so reckless? She had never engaged with a client like that before. What must he think of her? Her behavior had been so unprofessional.

Dani hadn't heard from Devon which in her mind meant he was done with her. As well, as he should be, she thought. The only drawback was, she had left her briefcase and sample case, at his house. Which meant, she would have to retrieve them. She couldn't bear the thought of having to face him again after her lustful behavior.

"Oh no, no, no. I CAN NOT GO BACK! I will just have to replace everything. I can afford it." Accepting this as her only solution, Dani started to feel a little better and finally relaxed.

Looking back on her conduct, she just couldn't understand what made her go that far with him. It all started as a game to her. She had no intention of letting it go as far as it had. But once he touched her, everything reasonable left her.

Her with her big mouth. Why did she have to challenge him, by asking him, "what he wanted to do about those feelings?" And why did she get so emotional at the thought of losing him, when she didn't even have him? She just could not understand why her emotions were all over the place.

"Good morning Dani," Andee greeted her as she breezed into her office with the morning's messages.

"Hi, Andee." She replied dryly.

"What's the matter, Sis? You look tired. Are you not sleeping well?" Andee asked her concerned.

"I'm fine girl. I just have a lot on my mind is all." Dani tried to gather some strength to endure her day.

"Is there anything important that I have to take care of today? Any clients I need to see or houses to decorate?"

"Nooo," Andee answered, puzzled. "I thought you were working on a new project?" She asked her, still perplexed.

"Oh, that fell through," Dani dismissed with a wave of her hand. "The client changed his mind. He decided to put it off for later, so I'm free for the next few days."

Not able to meet Andee's eyes, Dani rambled on. "I guess I will just take this time to do some buying, to replenish our inventory."

"Ok," Andee replied suspiciously, not knowing what to think. Something was wrong. Something, that Dani did not want to talk about—at least not now anyway.

"Oh, I almost forgot," Andee remembered, slapping her forehead with her palm. "You did have a call from a Mr. Powers. He asked if you were in. I offered to put him through, but he said that it wasn't necessary and hung up," she concluded, with a shrug.

"Do you know him?" Andee pressed. She had a feeling, that whatever was bothering Dani, this Powers person was a big part of it.

"Did he say what he wanted?" Dani asked, deflecting her question.

"No. He just asked if you were in is all."

"Ok, thanks," Dani replied, still not able to meet Andee's eyes.

She couldn't. Andee was very perceptive when it came to her and Paige. She couldn't look at her, for fear Andee would see her shame.

"Well, if you want to talk, you know I'm here for you," Andee added, before leaving Dani to her thoughts.

Dani didn't reply. She was deep in thought, trying to figure out, why Devin called, but didn't want to speak with her. She could only imagine the worst.

"Well, I can't sit here all day worrying. I may as well get some work done." She turned to her computer screen, to pull up some websites.

She was searching an auction site, to find some unique pieces to add to her inventory, when she felt a presence in her doorway. Dani looked up to find Devin standing there, with a huge bouquet of exotic flowers. She didn't know what to say. Dropping her head, she couldn't look at him without feeling ashamed.

"May I come in?" Devin asked.

Dani nodded.

"Your assistant said it would be ok for me to come to your office," he added, closing her door.

"I left the things you abandoned at my house with her."

"Devin I…" Dani began, still not managing to look him in the eye.

"Don't apologize. You don't have anything to apologize or feel embarrassed for," he assured her.

"How can you say that after how I behaved?" Dani responded, this time peering up at him for only a second.

"It was completely unprofessional. I have never done anything like that before in my life," she continued, closing her eyes and shaking her head.

"I just don't know what came over me. You must be disgusted with me. I wouldn't blame you if you were."

Devin realized, that he was going to have to take this situation into his own hands, to get her to look at him. To get her to understand what was happening between them. He placed the bouquet on her desk, then walked around it to pull her to her feet.

"Look at me, Dani. Baby, please look at me."

Reluctantly, Dani raised her eyes to him.

"Does it look like I am disgusted or put off by you? I could never feel anything but love for you. It may sound strange, but I do love you. I think that you felt that when we made love."

Dani looked at him for the first time, with uncertainty at what he was saying.

"Yes, Dani. We made love, it was not just sex. I can understand that it may have frightened you. Not by what I just said, but by your feelings."

She was confused. What was he talking about? She didn't know what she was feeling, or what to think. How could he be so certain?

"How can you be so sure? You're not confused?" She asked him.

"No baby I'm not. I knew the moment you felt it, felt what I was feeling. I saw it in your eyes. I didn't come after you right away, because I knew you needed some time to process what was happening. So stop beating yourself up. You did nothing wrong. It was meant to be."

"Devin we just met, we shouldn't be feeling this way." Dani wanted to believe him, but it was too soon.

"Who can put a timeline on love? But I must admit, if someone had told me there was such a thing as love at first sight, I wouldn't have believed them. That was before I met you. Come here"

Devin pulled Dani into his arms and kissed her. She wrapped her arms around him pulling him closer, wishing that she could have more of him. They kissed, for what seemed like an eternity, before they parted for air.

"Do you trust me?"

Dani answered him with a nod of her head.

"I won't ever hurt you, Dani, because I do love you," Devin lovingly reassured her.

"Now that we have that settled. Can I expect you at my house later?"

Dani laughed. "I guess I do have a job to finish. I will see you a little later."

"Oh Devin…" She continued hesitantly. "I know you said that you didn't want anyone to know…"

"Well, I guess that cat is out of its bag, with me showing up here, with flowers no less. Oh well," he shrugged. "I knew I would have to share you sooner or later." He grinned with a wink. After kissing her once more, Devin left.

He had barely cleared the building when both Andee and Paige came rushing into her office. Both women ask questions at once. Dani just shook her head, laughing at the perplexed expressions on their faces.

"Hold on. One question at a time please."

"Who was that?" Andee was the first to ask.

"His name is Devin Powers."

"Devin Powers?! The multimillionaire Devin Powers, who just recently moved to Metro City, Devin Powers?" Paige asked in disbelief.

"Yes, the one and only" Dani answered.

"Paige, were you here when he arrived?" Dani asked, folding her arms with a smirk.

Looking sheepish, Paige admitted that she had just gotten there. Andee had met her at the door, to tell all about the gorgeous man, who had shown up with flowers to see Dani. Andee had also speculated, that he was the source of Dani's sour mood she had been in earlier.

"How did you meet him?" Andee and Paige asked simultaneously.

"Well, Andee, do you remember the woman who called a couple of weeks ago, that insisted on speaking with me directly?"

Andee nodded that she did.

"Devin was the client, who she was calling for."

Dani went on to explain how she came to meet Devin, and why she didn't tell them she was working on his home.

"I want to know what he did wrong to show up here with dozens of flowers," Andee asked curiously.

"Well actually...he didn't do anything wrong. I was the one in the wrong, or so I thought."

Reluctantly, Dani explained what had taken place between her and Devin. She explained her embarrassment, and the mixed emotions that she had concerning him.

"Wow! Talk about a whirlwind romance," Paige was saying. "You certainly can't accuse him of dragging his feet, when it came to love. I am so happy for you. So, he asked if you trusted him, do you?" Paige asked.

"As strange as it may seem, I do. I have never felt this way about any man ever. I've been in serious relationships a couple of times, but never had feelings that ran that deep, in either of them."

"I'm happy for you too Sis." Andee joined in, hugging her.

"Well if you ladies will excuse me. I have a job to finish." Winking, Dani left them standing in her office.

Chapter 27

Anderson sat in the restaurant waiting for Mia to arrive. After speaking with her over the phone, he agreed to meet with her, as long as she was alone and not with Rendell.

He wondered about his newly found sister. What was she like? How was her childhood compared to his and Jayden's? He just couldn't think about his father having another family, without becoming angry. Angry for his mother and Jayden, but mostly angry for himself.

"Hi, Anderson. I'm sorry I'm late."

Caught up in his thoughts, Mia had slid into the booth, before Anderson realized she was there.

His sister. He just couldn't get over it. There she sat. Mia was a beauty no doubt. How could she be anything but, Anderson mused, she was a Stone. Her high cheekbones and reddish-brown coloring only added to her exotic features. She looked like a model.

"Not a problem," was all that Anderson could say at the moment. He still couldn't get a grip on how to proceed with his new sister. All of his training as a litigator did not prepare him for this moment. For a while, they just sat studying one another. Each recognizing their father in the other.

"I've talked to Jayden and he would very much like to meet you," Anderson spoke first.

"What about our father, Anderson? Does he want to meet him also?" Mia asked hopefully.

"Mia…" He paused. "You have to understand. Jayden knows nothing of the man, other than what he has learned from me and my mother. I don't know how he feels, other than he made no indication that he wanted to meet him. So I will have to say no."

Anderson watched her hope deflate. Anderson hated to be so blunt, but that was the reality of the situation.

Mia studied her brother. She was amazed by recognizing so much of their father in him, a younger version of Rendell. Although she understood his anger, she wanted Anderson to at least try to talk to him. She had high hopes that one day, Anderson could forgive their father for his sins.

No. She couldn't relate to the pain she saw in his eyes, brought on by Rendell's abandonment. She always had her father in her life. She just couldn't imagine what it was like, to grow up without him.

One thing Mia did know. Rendell was sorry for the choices that he made in the past. She remembered when she was old enough to understand, Rendell had revealed that she had two older brothers. When she asked where they were and if she could meet them, he told her of his selfish choice and of the pain that he caused his family. From that moment on, she had watched Rendell struggle with the guilt of leaving his pregnant wife and son behind.

After Rendell left Adaisha and Anderson, he moved to Phoenix to live with Mia's mother. He had met her on one of his many trips there and had fallen in love with her. A year after his divorce was final, he married her. Soon after the marriage, their son Kirby was born.

Kirby, born with multiple birth defects, had only lived two years before he died from complications of an enlarged heart. Rendell felt this was his punishment for leaving Adaisha, while she was carrying Jayden.

Two years later, his wife became pregnant again and Mia was born. Thanking God for a healthy happy baby, Rendell vowed, that given a chance, he would somehow make amends for his transgressions with his first family.

Mia knew the pain he struggled with. She watched him, whenever he read an article about Anderson or saw him on television in news clips. He was proud of his son's success. However, at the same time, saddened by the knowledge, that he had nothing to do with it. Adaisha had raised fine sons, and he, their father, could only watch them from afar.

Mia tried to convey all of this to her brother. To get him to see, that Rendell realized he had made a mistake. She needed Anderson to understand, that he would very much like to get to know the sons, whom he so selfishly turned his back on. But Mia pleaded Rendell's case to no avail. Anderson wasn't interested.

"I know that you love Rendell," Anderson told her. "It's evident in the way you speak of him and I don't want to take from that. I just don't want to have anything to do with the man. I'm sorry. I just hope that you won't hold that against me."

"Mia, Jayden, and I would like to get to know you and only you. Unlike Rendell, you have no blame in this situation. None of this is your fault."

Mia sighed deeply. She realized that the father-son reunion was not going to happen anytime soon. That she had to accept—at least for now. She was determined, whether Anderson liked it or not, to unite her family. Yes, she loved her father and she wanted to help him mend fences with his sons, her brothers. But for now, she would just have to settle for building her relationship with them.

After tabling the discussion about Anderson meeting with their father, the siblings ordered lunch and got acquainted.

Although Mia knew of him and Jayden, Anderson knew nothing of her. He learned that Mia was twenty-five years old, and had moved to Metro City, after college, to work as an accountant for one of the top advertising agencies in the country. She informed him, that her mother had died a few years back of breast cancer, and that it was just her and their father. He learned that the day he and Paige had encountered them, she and Rendell had stopped for a bite to eat. She explained that from there, she was taking him to the airport, after a weeklong visit. They had no idea, that Anderson had moved into the area.

After their meal, Anderson encouraged Mia to call Jayden. He sat there observing, as she heard her brother's voice for the first time. He watched a smile of wonderment grow on his sister's face, as she savored the moment of being in the presence of her two brothers.

Chapter 28

Rendell gently placed the receiver on its cradle, before he sat heavily into his chair. Mia had just informed him, that her brothers did not wish to meet with him. He knew this was a possibility, but he was hoping against hope, that she could talk them into meeting with him, if only briefly.

Rendell knew it was a long shot, but he had to try. He had to attempt to fix the mess that he had made so many years ago. Shaking his head, he wondered how he was going to put things back in order. How he was going to make amends. He needed his boys to know how deeply sorry he was, for the choices that he made. He had to make them understand that he paid for those choices each, and every day of his life. Sighing, Rendell closed his eyes, settled back into his comfortable chair, and traveled back to when he was cocky enough to think he knew everything. Back to the day that he lived to regret.

Rendell had stuffed his duffle bag with clothes and pulled it onto his shoulder. He did not look at his wife, because he didn't want to see the hurt in her eyes. The sobbing was bad enough. He threw one of his two bankbooks, on the bed and left. He told Adaisha that he didn't want to be a husband anymore. Although in truth, he didn't want to be her husband.

On his many trips out west for his job, he met Mia's mother Miranda. Miranda was twenty years old, beautiful, and adored him—or so he thought. After meeting Miranda, Rendell started spending all of his free time with her, whenever the job brought him to Arizona. Most of that time, they spent in bed, where she made him feel like the man he thought he was.

"How could I have been so stupid?" Rendell whispered into the air.

Getting up, he walked across the room to the bar, to pour himself a drink. Downing the expensive single malt scotch in one swallow, he continued to gaze back into the past.

Things were great with Miranda at first. As soon as he left Adaisha and Anderson, he immediately left the state, filed for divorce, and set up house with her. He made sure she had the finest of everything, and she loved every moment of it. She took care of home and him. Rendell was very happy.

However, as soon as his divorce was final and he married Miranda, that is when things began to change. When he was out on the rail line, she would be out having fun with other men; younger men; men her age. He hadn't known, until one day he overheard some of his coworkers commenting on, the "old fool" and the young girl. It hadn't taken him long to realize, they were referring to him. Especially, when the conversation dried up the moment he entered the room.

Rendell had confronted Miranda. They had argued bitterly, with her denying everything. Somehow she convinced him, that the men were just jealous, only wanting what he had. At the time, he didn't know, that some of them had sampled what he had. Miranda managed to smooth over his doubts, by coaxing him into bed. Soon all was forgotten. Things had gone back to the way they were before, him adoring her, she "adoring" him.

Days after their make-up, Miranda informed him that she was carrying his child. Although Rendell felt the child was his, he was torn by this new revelation. When he married Miranda, he wanted her, but not another child. On the other hand, he felt maybe a child would help his young wife to settle down. This was not to be so. Miranda quickly slipped back into her carefree ways.

When their son Kirby was born with multiple health problems and birth defects, this put even more strain on an already stressed marriage. Whereas Rendell spent most of his spare time caring for his son, Miranda was out shopping and hanging with her friends. He viewed his so-called marriage, plus his sickly child, as being his punishment, for his selfishness in leaving his first family. He thought about this, every time Miranda brought in more shopping bags, or when she came home just as the sun was rising. Claiming she had been out dancing with her girlfriends, whenever he questioned her behavior.

After Kirby died, Rendell considered divorcing Miranda and moving on. He knew he should have cut his losses, but his ego wouldn't allow him to. Therefore, he stayed to save face. To save face with whom, he didn't know; himself, his coworkers? He just couldn't give in to another failed relationship, even if it was of his own making.

Later, when Miranda became pregnant again with a healthy happy Mia, Rendell was determined to do right by this child. He took over completely. Becoming Mia's sole parent. Not that it mattered much to Miranda. She couldn't be bothered with raising a child. She had much more important things to do, like living a life of leisure. All in all, Rendell concluded, that Miranda never loved him. That she only loved the life that he afforded her. She was the total opposite of Adaisha.

Ah…Adaisha. His Adaisha. She loved him flaws and all. She made a real home for him and Anderson, but he threw it all away for a woman who would never love him. He didn't have to worry that Adaisha was out running around town with other men, while he was out on the job. She truly loved him, and it showed in how she viewed him, and in the way she responded to him. Especially, when they made love. Not like Miranda, who only fell into bed with him to get what she wanted.

Pouring another scotch, Rendell wished that he could go back in time and change the events, that had shattered his life, his family's lives. He thought about the selfishness, that took him from the love of a good woman. A woman he realized too late, that he should have loved and wanted.

Closing his eyes, he thought about how Anderson looked at him that day in the restaurant. He thought of the anger and hatred he saw in his son's eyes and how it had frightened him. He knew he had hurt him, but hadn't known to what extent, until that very moment. He was grateful Mia was with him. Had she not, he believed Anderson would have physically hurt him.

Mia, bless her heart, wanted so much for them all to be a family. After her mother died, she had asked him more about her brothers, his sons, whom he so callously threw away. Of Anderson, he could only tell her of the little boy of the past, not of the grown man that he had become today. This was because he had made the mistake of never contacting Adaisha or Anderson after the day he left. To learn of today's Anderson, unfortunately, he had to gather this information from the many news articles he had read on the internet. Anderson had become an accomplished attorney, a fine young man. Adaisha had done an excellent job in raising him.

Jayden was another story. Rendell was most ashamed when the subject of his younger son came up. He knew nothing of Jayden because he wasn't born until after he left. He didn't even know what his younger son looked like.

Feeling the pain of his actions, Rendell made a decision that could very well push him and his sons further apart, but he had to try. Reaching for the phone again, he punched in some numbers and made flight reservations.

Chapter 29

Adaisha Stone's brow furled when she heard the chimes of her doorbell.

"Now who could this be this late?" She mumbled under her breath with annoyance.

Adaisha had been relaxing in her media room, enjoying one of her favorite television shows, when the doorbell rang. Glancing at the clock, she pondered who could possibly be at her door. She knew that it wasn't Jayden, because he had been there earlier in the evening. Anderson wasn't in town, so that ruled him out. Her friends, knowing her routine, would never come calling at this hour, unless it was an emergency.

Making her way to the door, she paused momentarily, to check her appearance in the foyer's mirror. She ran a hand through her freshly styled bob, satisfied that she was presentable in her silk lounge attire with matching silk slippers. Still annoyed that her evening was interrupted, Adaisha opened the door to a man she never expected to see again—Rendell Stone.

"Hello, Adaisha," Rendell greeted with a small smile.

Rendell couldn't believe, that he was standing in front of the woman he abandoned so many years ago. He wasn't sure what he expected before she opened that door. Admittedly, a part of him wanted her to look a little worse for wear, waiting for him to return. What he saw before him was a woman who was relaxed, well-groomed, and glowing with health. She stood there in an expensive pale peach ensemble that was tailored to her sized six, well-toned body. Adaisha was as beautiful as she was the day she walked down the aisle to marry him.

Speechless, Adaisha stood there staring at the man who had walked out and broken her heart so many years ago. Her mind was racing, asking a hundred questions all at once. Pulling her thoughts to a complete stop, she folded her arms, raised an eyebrow, and asked the question that mattered the most.

"Rendell, what the hell do you want?"

\#

Adaisha sat at her kitchen's island, staring at the man, who nearly single-handedly, tried to destroy her life. Against her better judgment, she let Rendell into her home. She led him into her kitchen, where she offered him a seat and made tea. They exchanged small talk until the tea had finished brewing. She then joined him with a mug of green tea for each of them.

Sipping from her mug, she waited for him to explain why he was there. She watched him toy with his drink, trying to decide on how to proceed. Adaisha took this time to give her ex-husband the once over. She concluded that he hadn't changed much over the years. Aside from the gray at the temples and the round soft belly, he looked mostly the same. He was expensively dressed and groomed, so she assumed that his life went on as planned. So why would this man show up on her doorstep, after all these years? What did he want from her? Hadn't he taken enough from her, those many years ago?

Adaisha remembered all too well, what he had taken from her. For a short moment, he had taken her sense of self and security. He had taken her self-esteem. She thought she had been the perfect wife for him. How could he have said that he didn't want to be married anymore?

The day Rendell walked out of her and her sons' lives, Adaisha thought she would die. She was inconsolable. There she was, pregnant and alone. Sitting on the bed they had shared, sobbing. She hadn't realized Anderson was in the house until he came running into the bedroom, the moment Rendell left. He had hugged her.

Hugged her tight, trying to comfort her. All the while crying himself. Holding him while he cried, she felt her son's pain more so than her own.

At that moment, she knew she could not allow herself to succumb to the grief and self-pity, that she wanted so desperately to give in to. She had children to care for. So for that reason alone, she pulled herself together, mapped out a plan, and moved ahead with her life. She gave her boys the best that she could, with the resources that she had. She found a job, and a comfortable place to live, and she gave Anderson and Jayden all the love that she could muster. Their life was by no means easy, but they made it through—no thanks to the man sitting in her kitchen.

"I have no right to ask you for any kind of favors or help..." Rendell was saying, "...but I didn't know who else to turn to."

"And you turned to me because...?" Adaisha asked, clearly puzzled, but unmoved.

"I want to get to know my sons," Rendell blurted out, matter-of-factly.

Adaisha chuckled at first. Then laughed, until tears rolled down her cheeks. She could not believe, that this man dared to come into her home, wanting her help to reach *her* sons. After she gathered her composure, aided by a napkin she retrieved from the sidebar, Adaisha's amusement turned into white-hot anger.

"You have the balls to come to my home and speak to me about MY sons? Whom you so offhandedly threw away like trash?"

Shaking her head and gesturing towards him she asked, "Who are you?"

"No, no, no. Don't answer that. I know exactly who you are," Adaisha continued, raising her hand like a stop sign.

Not giving him a chance to answer, she plowed forward. "You are still the same selfish, son-of-a-bitch you've always been," she continued heatedly, leaving Rendell stunned.

"Let me guess," She added while vacating her chair to pace the floor. "You went to either Anderson or Jayden…or maybe both and they told you to go straight to hell. Then you come to me wanting me to help you?"

She suddenly stopped pacing, to place her hands on the countertop, to lean into Rendell.

"Well, my answer is the same as my sons'…GO TO HELL! AND GET OUT OF MY HOUSE!" Adaisha screamed at him, pointing in the direction of the door.

Rendell recoiled from Adaisha as though she had become a venomous snake. He gazed at her with new eyes. This was not the woman, whom he left pleading for him not to leave so many years ago. Before he arrived, he was certain, that Adaisha was still the same soft-spoken, mild mattered woman he had left behind. On the contrary, this woman was strong, confident, and determined. He had made a mistake in coming there.

Rendell slowly rose from his chair, back peddling as he hurried from her home. Not sure what this new Adaisha was capable of, he wasn't about to turn his back on her.

Adaisha stood in her kitchen, staring at the space that her ex-husband had just departed from. When she heard her door close, she quickly moved to make sure that he was gone and her door was securely locked. Assuring herself that this was done, she pressed her back against the door, still seething with anger.

She hadn't thought about Rendell Stone in years. She hadn't seen him since the day that he left. Adaisha realized, that she had never dealt with her anger until now. She thought she had dealt with all of her feelings toward Rendell years ago. She now understood, she had dealt with every emotion, except the anger. Seeing him after all those years, coupled with his outrageous request, had pulled out the rage she hadn't even known existed inside of her. And she had plenty to be angry about.

Adaisha knew Anderson had located his father after he left law school, although he had never mentioned it to her. She had overheard a conversation, that he had with a private investigator, once when he visited her. Adaisha had waited for him to tell her about the search, but he never did. Therefore, out of curiosity, she launched an investigation of her own later.

Adaisha learned of Rendell's other life—the life he had with a much younger wife. She had been floored upon learning this information. He had told her he didn't want to be married when the truth was, he didn't want to be married to her. Adaisha remembered how she felt after she obtained that bit of news. That old sense of insecurity had come rushing back, along with the self-doubt.

Looking at her reflection once more in the entryway mirror, she smiled. Never again, she assured herself. It had taken time and a lot of therapy, but she was past the days of Rendell Stone and his betrayal. Despite him, she had become the self-confident woman who had ordered him out of her home. Taking a last, confident look at her image, Adaisha pushed away from the door and went to bed.

#

Driving back to the airport in his rental, Rendell pounded the steering wheel. His chances of reconciling with his sons didn't look good. He was sure Adaisha would help him. The woman he knew in the past, would not have held a grudge. He hadn't expected the anger, that she had displayed, nor the indifference that radiated from her the moment she opened the door. He had hoped that she still had some feelings for him, and would be eager to help. He had made a mistake.

Chapter 30

It was a couple of days before their trip and Paige was ecstatic. It seemed the days were dragging by. She looked forward to spending some time with her man. Her man, that sounded good and Anderson was all hers.

She only heard from Justin once more during that week. He called professing his love for her. Telling her he couldn't give up because she was his soul mate. She only rolled her eyes at his latest attempt and again asked him to stop calling her and to be sure that he didn't, she blocked his number on her mobile phone.

Andee, after learning Justin had tried to slither back into Paige's life, decided to do a little investigative work of her own. She found, that not only was Justin not getting a divorce, but that he had no intentions of getting one. He loved the lifestyle that his wife's money afforded him. The man was a lying snake after all. This was of no consequence to Paige, for her heart belonged solely to Anderson.

#

"Are you ready for your trip?" Dani was asking Paige.

"Girrlll, just a few more things to pack, then Aruba here we come," Paige answered while doing a little dance in Dani's office.

"Well, I'm just going to let you know that I'm jealous. All that sun and fun…I wish I were going," Andee chimed in.

"Maybe if you're a good girl, Jayden will take you on a trip. How is the great romance going by the way?" Paige inquired.

Andee did her best to put on a happy smile. She and Jayden had been spending a lot of time together, alternating weekends to see each other. She was head over heels. However, her last trip to visit Jayden had left a lot to be desired. She was still upset about what happened one night, at his home with that woman. Although Jayden tried several times to talk to her, to explain, she wasn't ready to hear it.

"It's going just fine." She replied saying nothing more.

"Ok Missy, keep your secrets," Paige added laughing.

"Oh let's leave her alone. She will tell us when there is something to tell," Dani defended.

"Are you ladies sure, that you can hold things down while I'm gone?" Paige asked her two best friends. Oblivious to the pain that Andee fought hard to mask.

"Will you just go have some fun and not think about this place for a week? We have everything under control. Right, Dani?" Andee assured her with Dani nodding her agreement.

"Well if that's the case, I will see you ladies in a week." Hugging her friends, Paige left to start her vacation with Anderson.

After Paige left, Andee went back to her desk and thought about what she was going to do about Jayden. She just couldn't discuss their relationship with her friends. Especially now with the strain between them.

After meeting him, she was sure that he was the one for her. But now, she didn't know if that was still true. When she first met him, he explained that he was seeing someone back home and that it wasn't anything serious. Although, after her last visit, she wasn't quite sure he was telling the truth.

#

Jayden had picked her up from the airport, as he had done many times before. From there, they went to a local

Italian restaurant for dinner that evening. Everything was fine until they got back to his house. She and Jayden had just gotten settled on his sofa, preparing to watch a movie, when the doorbell rang.

"Are you expecting someone?" Andee asked him.

"No. I'm not. Maybe they will catch a hint and go away if I don't answer the door." That was not to be so. Whoever it was, continued to ring the doorbell.

"It's probably one of the guys from the fire department. I'll be right back."

Sighing, Jayden got up to get rid of the person, who dared to continue to lean on his doorbell.

Andee, thinking that Jayden had everything under control, settled back to enjoy the movie when he returned. But after he didn't return immediately, she got up to see what was keeping him. Making her way to the partially opened door, she found Jayden standing outside, speaking in hushed tones, to a very angry woman. He was trying to plead with the woman, but she was not having any of it.

"Jayden, is everything ok?" Andee asked him after stepping outside.

"Is that her? Is that the bitch you thought you would drop me for…huh?" The angry woman asked Jayden.

"DeLisa, don't do this," Jayden responded, in a low threatening tone.

"And who are you anyway?" DeLisa asked, completely ignoring Jayden.

Andee, who was never one to back down from a fight, prepared to do battle with the woman if necessary. One thing was for sure, she wasn't going to be too many more bitches. Despite the fact, that she didn't fully understand what was happening, she would take this woman down.

"The question is, who are you and what is this all about?" Andee asked the belligerent woman.

"I'm Jayden's fiancée...bitch. That's who I am," DeLisa announced, while gladly displaying her engagement ring to Andee.

Too stunned over the woman's claim, and the engagement ring on her finger, Andee didn't seem to take notice of DeLisa calling her bitch a second time. Looking to Jayden for an explanation and not readily getting one, Andee turned on her heels and headed back inside.

"Andee wait!" Jayden called after her.

Andee didn't stop. She kept right on walking. She heard Jayden tell his "fiancée" to leave and that he would deal with her later. She heard the woman respond, that she would be waiting and that she would forgive him, provided he got rid of "the bitch".

She didn't hear anymore, because she was too busy ordering an Uber to take her to the airport. She was going home. Finding what she was looking for, Andee tapped in Jayden's address and her destination.

Jayden found her in his bedroom, repacking the clothes that she had not an hour ago unpacked. She had even cleared out the clothes, that she left in his closet from previous visits.

"You said that it wasn't serious Jayden! But that woman's engagement ring says differently!" Andee screamed at him. One thing was for sure, she would not let him have the satisfaction of seeing her cry, she vowed.

"Andee baby wait! It's not what it looks like. I am not engaged to that woman!" Jayden pleaded, trying to stop her from packing her clothes.

"Then where did she get the ring Jayden? Huh? The ring that she was all too proud to show off!" She asked him.

"I don't know! She borrowed it... bought it... hell, all I know is I didn't give it to her!" He said pointing to himself.

At that moment, her phone chimed, indicating her Uber was outside.

"Right on time," Andee stated as she closed her suitcase.

"Right on time for what...what's going on Andee?"

Jayden grabbed her arm, as he tried to stop her from walking around him to get to the door.

"That's my ride," She retorted, snatching her arm from him. "You better go. Your "fiancée is waiting."

With that. She walked out his door, got into the car, and left.

Jayden couldn't believe what just happened. He wasn't engaged to DeLisa. The woman was delusional. Sure he had dated her. But after a month, he was sure that she was not the one for him and broke it off. She was rude, loud, and all around ghetto. He explained to her that they were too different and that it wasn't working for him. He thought she understood until a couple of weeks ago, when she showed up at his home out of the blue, wanting to give it another try. He firmly but gently told her that wasn't going to happen. Asking her not to come back. Jayden was sure that was the end of the situation. But here he was. Standing in his bedroom alone, after Andee walked out on him.

"I cannot believe this is happening!" Jayden shouted to the empty room.

Pacing back and forth, he knew he had to get this straightened out and fast. He could not lose Andee over some foolishness. Making up his mind, he grabbed his keys. He was going to put a stop to this nonsense once and for all!

#

Sitting at the gate waiting for her flight, Andee wiped tears from her eyes. She could not believe, Jayden had lied to her about something, that was so important. She thought back to the incident that occurred at his home. There was that woman, standing there with a smirk on her face, proudly displaying her engagement ring. She thought about the woman herself. She was so unlike anyone, that she would have thought Jayden would be involved with. She carried herself like a hood rat. He never came off as someone who would want that type of woman. And why had she not been aware of her before? Andee had been to Jayden's many times since meeting him. Not one time had there been any phone calls or visits from any women. A few of his buddies from the department had come by, but that was it. It didn't make sense. But on the other hand,

Justin hid his infidelity from Paige pretty well. So why couldn't Jayden have done the same thing?

Hearing her flight being called, Andee wiped away the last of her tears and prepared to board the plane.

Chapter 31

Stepping off the shuttle at their hotel, Paige took note of her surroundings.

"Anderson, it's beautiful here," She stated joyously.

Anderson agreed. He planned to keep her happy and entertained, every moment they were there. Kissing her, they headed to the front desk to check in.

While Anderson retrieved their key cards, Paige ventured among the shops and boutiques in the lobby.

Browsing in one shop, she had the distinct feeling that she was being watched. She scanned the store, searching for the source of that feeling. Finding nothing, she decided she should return to Anderson just the same. Feeling more and more uncomfortable by the minute, Paige hurried to reach the front desk. In her haste, she rounded a corner and bumped directly into Anderson.

"Whoa! Are you alright?" Anderson asked, reaching out to steady her.

Not wanting to alarm him, Paige decided to keep her unease to herself. "Yes. I'm just ready to get this vacation started. What shall we do first?" She asked, smiling up at him.

"First my dear, we are going to get our things settled in our suite. Then we can decide from there."

Taking her hand, they headed for the elevator. Neither noticed the figure that stood in the massive lobby watching them.

#

After poring over the many brochures for activities that the island had to offer, Anderson and Paige decided to do some sightseeing before having a late lunch. They chose a guided tour, that took them through a jungle-like terrain, which displayed the beauty of the island. They viewed exotic animals in their natural habitat, along with crystal blue waterfalls that threatened to leave them breathless. They browsed craft markets and shops that boasted the best of the island's local flavor. Anderson helped Paige choose souvenirs for Andee and Dani before they decided to lunch at one of the island's most popular spots.

The restaurant they chose, specialized in Brazilian as well as other South American dishes. Anderson didn't know what to order first. He wanted a taste of everything, to help him concoct his unique versions when he returned home.

"Wow, what a meal," Anderson exclaimed, patting his flat abs as they headed back to the hotel. "If we eat like that every day we're here, I am going to gain twenty pounds."

Laughing Paige agreed. "You should have seen your face tasting each entrée. You looked as if you were a kid in a candy store, ready to eat everything in sight."

"Well Miss, you did quite a bit of damage there yourself." Justin teased.

"Yes. yes, I couldn't help myself. The food was delicious and I enjoyed every bite. Although, I still rate your meals as the best baby," Paige endeared with a kiss.

"So what would you like to do now my lady? Your wish is my command."

"Why don't we check in at one of the spas for a massage? Then maybe a nap before dinner?" Paige suggested.

"Sounds like a plan." Kissing her hand, Anderson led the way.

They spent the rest of the afternoon being pampered. Paige opted for the full spa package that included a total body treatment, along with a facial, manicure, and pedicure. Anderson chose a more basic package of a massage only. Leaving him enough time to shop and set up for a surprise he planned for Paige, later that week.

Later, after taking care of his plans, Anderson let himself into their suite, to find a smiling and glowing Paige, lying seductively on their bed, with every inch of her displayed. Obeying his body's command, Anderson hurriedly discarded his clothes to join her. He had barely touched the bed before he was inside of her. Moving with a hunger only she could stir in him. He rode her uncontrollably. Taking everything she had to offer. They both cried out. Surprised by the intensity of their joining. Anderson felt he could conquer anything at that moment. He couldn't get enough of her. It was as if he were an addict, and she was his addiction.

#

Waking to the sound of a ringing phone, Anderson rolled over to answer it. It was the six am wake-up call he requested. Although they had planned an evening of dinner and dancing the night before, they never left the room. After making love several more times that evening, they decided on room service and each other instead. Neither one of them wanted to venture outside of their love for each other.

Rolling back over to Paige, Anderson kissed her awake.

"Good morning baby," he greeted her; kissing her shoulder, and her back.

Paige moaning, turned towards Anderson, kissing him on the lips.

"What time is it?" She asked.

"It's time for us to get up if we're going to get some snorkeling and some more sightseeing in before lunch. But if you keep looking at me that way, we won't make it out of this bed," Anderson teased.

"I'll tell you what. I'll race you to the shower." Paige leaped from the bed and sprinted towards the bathroom.

#

After breakfast, Paige and Anderson spent the day beach hopping. Taking advantage of most of the aquatic activities that were offered. They enjoyed the beautiful coral world of multicolored fish and amazing blue water as they snorkeled. Later, Anderson convinced Paige to parasail; an adventure that literally and figuratively took her to new heights. They explored the sea shops for special treasures to add to their collection of island memories. They ended their beach adventure by dining at a seaside eatery.

The couple spent the rest of their vacation touring the island's museums and historic sites. They enjoyed learning about the history and culture of the people who lived there. They took plenty of photos and videos to document their time together in such a beautiful place. While part of their nights were spent, enjoying the island's nightlife of music and dancing, the other part was spent making love to the rhythm of their song.

#

It was there last night in Aruba and Anderson was nervous. He had planned everything down to the last detail. Wanting everything to be perfect. Dressed for dinner, he waited for Paige out on the balcony, rehearsing his speech again. Hoping that he wasn't so nervous, that he would forget what he planned to say. He loved Paige. Loved her enough to spend the rest of his life showing her how much.

Indicating that she was ready to leave, Anderson escorted her downstairs to the restaurant. Upon arriving, the maître d immediately escorted the couple to their table.

Paige looked around the expensive restaurant impressed. When Anderson requested that they dress eloquently for dinner, she had no idea that they would be dining at one of the most posh restaurants on the island. Their meal, which Anderson requested in advance, consisted of seven delicious courses. All were accompanied by the finest of wines. Paige was captivated.

"Anderson, what's going on here?" She inquired.

After they finished their meal, she noticed some of the other guests appeared to be observing them. Smiling as if they knew something she didn't. Unknown to her, the other patrons had been informed that the couple would be celebrating a special moment that night.

Anderson took this as his queue, to reveal the purpose of the special night.

"My love, it's our last night here and I wanted it to be one of the most memorable times of our lives. I love you, Paige Bennett," Anderson declared while continuing on bended knee.

"When you came into my life, you brought a joy that I didn't know existed. Loving you has been the high point of my life and I can't imagine another day without you."

Reaching into his jacket pocket, he pulled out a small black velvet box, opening it to display the most beautiful diamond ring, Paige had ever seen.

"Paige, will you marry me?"

Paige was beside herself. The other patrons seemed to be holding their breath, waiting for her answer.

With tears streaming down her face, she finally answered, "Yes!"

The room exploded with cheers and applause. Anderson stood, pulling Paige up into his arms, kissing her, not caring who was watching. And someone was watching from across the room—Justin Graham. And he wasn't pleased with the happy occasion.

Having gotten the best answer of his life, Anderson took his new fiancée back to their suite to continue the celebration. When they stepped inside the room, Paige was amazed at what she saw. Anderson had arranged for the bedroom to be transformed into a romantic paradise. White candles were lit around the room, giving it a soft inviting glow. The space had been filled with dozens of pale peach roses, Paige's favorites. There was champagne cooling, along with an assortment of foods, that included, white chocolate dipped strawberries, canapés and prawns. Also some of Paige's favors. Anderson wanted this night to be a night, that she cherished for the rest of her life.

"Anderson I am so happy. I didn't dare believe that I could be this happy, ever." Paige kissed him excitedly.

After Justin, she never thought that she would find a man, that would love her as much as Anderson. He made her feel as if she were the most important woman on the planet.

"Baby, I love you. There isn't anything that I wouldn't do to keep that smile on your face. You have made me the happiest man on this island tonight. I can't wait to be your husband."

Taking her face into his hands, Anderson kissed her, caressing her tongue with his. Paige moaned her answer.

Wanting to feel his hands on her skin, she gently pushed away and slowly began to undress. Taking her time. Watching him as she did so. Anderson seemed mesmerized, as she walked toward him. She then slowly helped him out of his jacket. She then proceeded, without hurry, to undo each button on his shirt. Anderson, wanting her to do what she willed to him, was having a difficult time keeping his hands from ripping the shirt off of his back. Finally, having removed his shirt, Paige removed his belt, and then his pants. Reaching inside his briefs, she found her treasure and slowly kneaded him.

Anderson, not able to stand it any longer, removed the final restraint. Lifting her into his arms, he quickly moved them to the bed. Not wanting to wait another second, he joined them with one swift stroke. The sudden contact made them both cry out with pleasure.

Anderson moved inside her. Feeling every ounce of love that he held for her. With each thrust, he consumed more and more of her. Feeling her love for him ebb and flow, as if she were melting, becoming a part of his own body. Anderson couldn't believe the intensity of them together. It took him beyond anything that he had ever known. Beyond anything he could have ever imagined. Feeling Paige tighten around him signaling her arrival, Anderson let go to join her. All the while, professing his love for her.

#

Later after they had showered together, Paige and Anderson sat out on the balcony. Enjoying their last night in Aruba, toasting their engagement. Lost in each other, they did not hear the door to their suite open and close, as Justin let himself into their room.

After witnessing Paige and Anderson's engagement, he had sat at the bar drinking. Trying to drown his misery. He had followed them to Aruba, in hopes of getting Paige alone, to make her see that she would always belong to him. When he learned she was seeing Anderson he wanted her back. It didn't matter that he was married. He vowed that he would find a way to work around that.

So after drinking enough liquid courage, he decided he would confront Paige. He had to convince her, that she belonged with him. He bribed one of the attendants at the front desk for a keycard.

"You can't marry him, Paige. You're mine!" Justin proclaimed when he reached them.

Startled upon hearing his voice, both Paige and Anderson stood to their feet.

"Justin, what are you doing here?" Paige asked, clearly stunned.

"What are you doing here Graham?" Anderson asked through clenched teeth while taking a step towards him.

"I came for my woman. I came for you, Paige." Ignoring Anderson, Justin reached for Paige.

"You know you still love me, Paige," Justin slurred, trying to pull her into his arms.

Before he could accomplish this, Anderson punched him in the mouth. Justin, even in his drunken state, charged Anderson.

The two men fought, while Paige rushed inside to call for help.

"Please send security, there is an intruder in our room! Hurry, please!" Paige spoke quickly, informing the front desk of the trouble in their suite.

By the time security had reached their room, Anderson had subdued Justin, holding him until he could be carted off to jail. Justin, having had all the fight taken out of him, Justin hung his head as he was escorted from the room.

"Will you be pressing charges?" Asked the head of security.

"Yes, we will," answered Anderson, holding a shaken Paige. "I need to have this incident documented, in case he tries something like this again, or worse."

"Yes sir. I will send the police up as soon as they arrive, so you may make a formal complaint. Good night Sir, Miss." The man nodded to each of them.

"Baby, are you alright?" Anderson held Paige tighter after the room was clear.

"I'm fine...Anderson, you're bleeding!" Paige noticed he had a split lip.

"It's fine baby. He got one lucky punch in that's all. I'll be ok." He rubbed her back reassuring her.

"What is wrong with that man? How could he come here and do this?" Paige asked, puzzled.

"I don't know baby. But he confirmed what we thought. He wanted back into your life. I had a feeling that we would be seeing him again. But never in my wildest dreams would I have thought he would have shown up here," Anderson continued, shaking his head in disbelief.

"Anderson?" Paige asked.

"Hmm?"

"Do you think we can leave a little earlier?" Paige was more than ready to leave after Justin's unhinged interruption.

"Not a problem. Why don't you get dressed and get us packed? I will go downstairs and take care of everything."

With that settled. They kissed and parted, each to their agreed-upon tasks.

Chapter 32

"Andee please let me in," Jayden pleaded outside of Andee's door.

"I can explain everything if you would just open the door and let me in."

Andee stood pressed against the other side of the door. Listening to Jayden plead. She wanted to let him in, but she didn't want to hear any lies from him. On the other hand, she knew she needed answers. Sighing deeply, she opened the door.

Jayden stood there looking lost and defeated. He looked as if he hadn't slept in days. From the growth on his face, he hadn't shaved in a few days. That was for certain.

"Can I come in?" He asked when she didn't invite him in.

Opening the door wider, Andee allowed him to enter. Closing the door behind her, she followed him to her sofa.

"You said you can explain. So let's hear it."

Jayden had tried several times to explain to Andee, what happened with DeLisa and why, but she wasn't hearing it. Each time that he called her to explain, she would either not answer or would hang up each time she heard his voice. He knew how bad things looked that night she walked out on him, but it was all a setup. He needed to make sure that she knew that.

"As I told you before you left, I had only dated DeLisa a month before I realized that she was not the woman for me. I thought I'd made it plain to her that I didn't want to see her again, but she had other ideas. She thought by showing up when she did, that she would scare you away and that I would in turn be with her. After you left I went straight to the police station to get a restraining order against her. And it was a good thing that I did. When I didn't show up at her place, she bee-lined it back to my house. This time she wasn't so nice."

"What happened?" Andee asked, still skeptical.

"Andee, the woman put on a show. She started by throwing rocks. Breaking as many windows as she could. Baby, the woman is insane. She cursed and screamed until some of the neighbors finally called the cops. I found out later that she was bipolar and she had stopped taking her medication. After the rock-throwing incident at my house, her sister came by the firehouse to apologize for her behavior. She told me that DeLisa had taken her engagement ring and was pretending that she and I were engaged. Here is all the documentation of everything that I just told you."

Jayden pulled some papers out of his back pocket and handed them to her. Andee took the papers and thumbed through them. There were police reports taken on the night that she left, along with the restraining order that he had gotten.

"Jayden, I don't know what to say. I should have believed you when you said you weren't engaged to her. I should have known better. Out of all the times that I've been at your place, that was the only time a woman ever showed up. You never had any calls from females other than your mother. Can you forgive me for not believing you?" Andee asked of him remorsefully.

"Baby there is nothing to forgive. I later realized that had the tables been turned, I would not have believed you either. I mean, the woman was convincing. And I didn't make it any better, by not answering you right away. It was just that…that, I was so surprised by her tactics, I was speechless. I'm the one who's sorry. I should have known that something was wrong when the woman wouldn't take no for an answer the first time she showed up at my house."

"Shhh…no more talk about that crazy woman,"
Andee whispered, taking his face into her hands.

"I have missed you so much," she added before
kissing him.

Jayden picked her up and carried her to her
bedroom.

#

"I cannot believe that fool dared to show up on your
vacation," Andee was saying, in disbelief.

"Paige you had to be terrified," Dani added.

"It was pretty scary. There we were enjoying our
last night and in pops Justin out of nowhere." Paige was
still finding it difficult to believe what Justin did.

"I was so glad that Anderson was there. I don't
know what he would have done, had I been there alone."
Paige shuddered at the thought; hugging herself.

They were sitting in Paige's living room. Andee and
Dani had rushed right over after learning of the incident
during the society segment of the local morning show.
Somehow, the news of Justin's arrest had made it across
the ocean and hit the headlines. The host revealed in detail,
the altercation that led to his arrest. The co-host speculated
over what actions Justin's wife, Anastasia Stanton-Graham,
would be taking. Considering he had embarrassed the

Stanton family. The host further speculated, that there may be a divorce in Justin Graham's near future.

"We're just glad that you and Anderson are safe. It could have been worse than what it was," Dani speculated.

"Hey, where is Anderson?" Andee asked Paige.

"He went to the local precinct to file the paperwork on Justin. Just in case he decides to give us a repeat performance."

"I don't think that you have to worry about Mr. Justin Graham anymore," Andee offered.

"I believe his wife will make sure he never bothers you again. Even though social media commenters hinted, that there could be a divorce, either way, I am pretty sure Anastasia Stanton-Graham will make his life a living hell. He won't have the time or the energy to bother you again," she added with a satisfied grin.

"Well enough on that. Let's get to the good part. How was the vacation? What all did you do and see?" Dani prompted.

"Oh, we had a wonderful time. There was snorkeling, parasailing, and you know our passion for museums. We took plenty of pictures and…Oh, I almost forgot! We got engaged!" Paige screamed this last part, showing them the ring she had been hiding on her finger.

Dani and Andee both screamed their surprise and excitement.

"Paige…oh it's beautiful," Dani complimented.

"I'm so happy for you," Andee added, hugging her.

"We both are," Dani beamed.

"Thank you ladies. I am so excited."

Paige shared the romantic details that Anderson had arranged for their special night. She told them, how everyone in the restaurant was in on the night. How surprised and excited that she was. She also explained, that it was after they had gotten back to their suite, when Justin showed up drunk.

"So Anderson beat him up. I would have paid good money to see that. He got what he deserved." Andee high-fived Dani laughing.

"Yes, he was a pretty sorry sight when the police arrived to cart him off to jail. I can't believe that I ever loved him." Paige shook her head with wonder.

"Hey. That was not your fault. The man is a narcissistic fool. I mean, who does he think he is, insisting that you were his?" Dani was annoyed at the man's audacity.

"Enough talk about that idiot. Let's talk wedding dresses," Paige suggested.

Chapter 33
Six months later

Paige stood in the dressing room peering into the floor-length mirror, turning from one side to the other. She was in awe of the reflection she saw there. She was beyond happy, dressed in a beautiful designer silk gown, a gift from her soon-to-be mother-in-law. Dani had applied her make-up and Andee helped her with her hair. She felt blessed to have such good friends.

"Is Devon going to make it to the ceremony?" Paige asked Dani, while still admiring her reflection.

"I just spoke with him. His flight just left. He won't make the wedding but will be at the reception for sure. He asked that I give you his regrets. It just couldn't be helped." Dani answered shrugging.

Devon was out of town on business and was delayed by the weather, preventing him from attending the wedding.

"You two have been almost inseparable since you met. Love looks good on you Dani," Andee commented.

"I do love him, but girl..." Dani replied shaking her head... "I am still trying to wrap my head around this love-at-first-sight thing that he insists is a thing."

"Could it be, we will be attending another wedding soon?" Paige inquired, turning towards Dani with a raised brow.

"Even though we love each other, we are taking it slow, as we should. We still have a lot to learn about one another. I for one, want to be certain that he is the "one", Dani replied with air quotes. She understood Devins's point of view, but she wanted to feel completely secure in her choice of committing to him for life.

"Good for you," Paige remarked.

"So Andee, is everything good with you and Jayden? Any more deranged women showing up on his doorstep?" Dani asked.

Andee finally shared with them the incident with DeLisa at Jayden's.

"All is well," Andee chuckled. "Although, looking back on that night, deranged or not, I still owe that woman a beat down for calling me a bitch."

The friends laughed.

"And speaking of women, I finally got a chance to meet Mia. She is so much like Jayden and Anderson. I like her," Andee added.

"Yeah, I do too. She is a lovely young woman and her brothers adore her as if they all grew up together," Paige replied.

"I just wish the brothers could work things out with their father. Anderson made it clear to Mia, that she was welcome to come to the wedding, but under no circumstances would Rendell be allowed near the premises." Paige frowned. She wanted her Anderson to heal. In her opinion, that wouldn't happen until he confronts the problem with his father directly.

"Well, you never know. They may have a change of heart someday. People do change," Andee replied.

"Hey, has anyone heard the latest on Justin?" Dani inquired, looking from Paige to Andee.

"Surprisingly no. It's been quiet on that front. I'm surprised Anastasia has divorced his ass by now and ruined him in the process, but no such luck," Andee told them.

"Maybe she's one of those stand-by-your-man wives, who stick with their lying cheating husbands come what may," she added with a shrug.

"Well, enough on that. Could you ladies please help me with my veil? The wedding is about to start and I am anxious to become Mrs. Paige Stone," Paige interjected with a huge grin.

#

In the groom's dressing room, Adaisha straightened her Anderson's tie. "I am so proud of you son. Paige is a wonderful woman. I see why you love her so much. I can see she has a good heart." Adaisha hugged her son.

Letting go of her firstborn, Adaisha turned to her youngest. "Now. When will we be getting an announcement from you young man?"

"Well uh…" Jayden stammered. He wasn't expecting his mother to turn on him with hopes of matrimony for his future.

"I'm only teasing Jayden. Relax." Adaisha laughed while hugging a stunned Jayden.

"You should see your face little brother," Anderson chuckled.

"Yeah, well…" Jayden laughed nervously.

"I'm glad you decided to invite your sister to the ceremony, Anderson. She belongs here with her brothers," Adaisha interjected suddenly.

"Well, after you told us you knew about Rendell's family, there wasn't a reason not to," he replied.

Adaisha informed them how she had come about the knowledge of her former husband's family, but not about Rendell's late-night visit. She knew they would go ballistic. Rendall had caused enough drama with his reappears in their lives, she didn't want to add more fuel to that particular fire.

"Mom, we never wanted you to know how far he had gone in betraying you. You didn't deserve that," Jayden added.

"I know son. I must admit, when I first learned of his other family, I was hurt. But that was many years ago. That man has no hold on me anymore, and I thank God for it. Now, as for you boys, I cannot say the same. You will both have to deal with him in your way."

"Look, mom. This is my wedding day. Let's not turn this joyful occasion into a somber one by bringing up that old skeleton. Ok?" Anderson pleaded, just as the music began to play in the chapel, signaling that the wedding was about to begin.

#

Anderson stood at the altar with his brother Jayden, waiting for his beautiful bride to appear. Dani and Andee were coming down the aisle with radiant smiles, wearing the most elegant and beautiful of dresses. After Andee took her place, she and Jayden shared knowing smiles, both lost in each other.

Then the moment Anderson had waited for his entire life arrived. Paige, wearing a silver beaded white silk designer gown, was walking towards him. She was breathtaking. Her smile let him know that she loved and needed him just as much as he did her. He couldn't wait to become her husband.

#

The wedding reception was in full swing. The guests were having a wonderful time enjoying the fabulous food, drink, and music the happy couple had provided. Both Anderson and Paige's families were in attendance, along with their friends and clients. Paige even invited Jean, who was having a great time dancing with Paige's brother, Evan.

Paige, deciding to let bygones be bygones, had mended fences with her. She believed the woman just needed some genuine friends in her life. So she, along with Dani, and even Andee, started including her in some of their plans, and Jean was ecstatic.

"Congratulations Paige, hi Anderson. I just wanted to thank you both for inviting me to your wedding. I know I haven't been the friendliest person to you Paige, but I plan to make up for all that. I hope someday we all can be the best of friends," Jean gushed. She was the happiest she had been in a long time and she attributed her positive turn in life to Paige's influence.

"You're welcome, Jean. I would like that very much," Paige replied, hugging the woman.

"I see that you and my brother are getting along. He's a great guy. You can't go wrong with him. And I am not just saying that because he's my brother." Paige smiled. She genuinely hoped something wonderful could come from Jean and Evan's meeting.

Blushing, Jean replied, "He is sweet and I do like him."

"He seems to like you too. He asked about you, and don't worry, you have my blessing." Paige assured her that their past issues were just that the past.

"Thank you, Paige." Jean hugged her again, before floating off to find Evan.

"That was big of you my dear," Anderson stated, hugging his new bride.

"I think she just needs some caring people in her life. She doesn't want to be that mean and nasty woman she pretended to be."

Kissing her, Anderson was in heaven. He didn't know he could be this happy. His new wife was a remarkable woman. She was the one person that brought clarity to his life. Paige brought color, fun and most of all, the strongest love he has ever known.

"Hey break it up, break it up," Jayden joked, joining the couple.

"Congratulations guys. Paige, my new sister, you make a beautiful bride," Jayden complimented.

"Thank you, Jayden." She kissed his cheek.

"Well bro, what are you and Andee up to? I hear you two have been spending a lot of time together," Paige inquired of Jayden.

"Paige, your friend is one special woman and I do enjoy spending time with her. Who knows she may be the one," Jayden added with a wink and a grin.

"Good for you. I wish the two of you the best of luck." Paige was happy for them. "Where is Andee?"

"She's over there talking with our mother and your parents," Jayden answered thumbing toward the group.

"I see Devon made it to the reception," Anderson noted. He watched Devin join Dani and another couple. "He truly seems to love Dani. I recognize that look anywhere," he further noted.

"Yeah. You have that same look on your face right now," Jayden joked, with a chuckle.

"Umm…Don't look now guys, but it seems Mia has attracted every single male in the place," Paige informed her new husband and brother-in-law.

Glancing over to where Paige had indicated, the brothers saw that indeed, their baby sister was surrounded by a multitude of men.

"What the hell!" This didn't sit well with Jayden. "Oh no they don't," he added before marching off to play big brother, with Paige and Anderson laughing at his over-protectiveness.

"Ok, my lovely wife it's time that we left for our honeymoon," Anderson informed Paige by tapping at his watch.

Paige, gazing out over the crowd and at the events that brought her to this point, felt blessed that she finally possessed *The Touch of a man's heart.*

#

Unbeknownst to the reception's hosts and guests, Rendell watched the festivities from the shadowed background. He watched Jayden, the son he never knew, bully the young men away from his sister. Turning his attention to the happy couple, tears formed in his eyes for the family that he lost. The family that he threw away.

Lastly, letting his regrets settle on Adaisha, Rendell vowed to win his family back.